SIR WALTER SCOTT

IVANHOE

Retold by: Britt-Katrin Keson
Illustrations: County Studio, Beth Williamson
Series Editor: Paulette Møller

EASY CLASSICS

Editorial assistance:
Hanne Harboe, Aschehoug
Ulla Malmmose, Aschehoug

Cover layout: Jannie Andersen
Cover photo: From the motion picture
"Ivanhoe " © 1952
Turner Entertainment Co.
All rights reserved

Copyright: Aschehoug Dansk Forlag A/S, 1995
ISBN Denmark 87-11-09004-9

Printed in Denmark by
Sangill Bogtryk & offset, Holme Olstrup, 1995

SIR WALTER SCOTT
(1771-1832)

Sir Walter Scott was born in Edinburgh on August 15, 1771. Like his father, he studied law, but he soon discovered his passion for folklore and ballads, which he at first wrote as romantic poetry. In 1814, he started his career as a novelist with *Waverley*, the first of a series of novels set in his native Scotland including *Guy Mannering* (1815), *Old Mortality* (1816), and *The Heart of Midlothian* (1818). In 1819, Scott turned his attention to another popular folk story, *Ivanhoe*, probably his best-known novel. He was created baronet in 1820.

Throughout his life, Scott was fascinated by history and antiques, and in 1812 he built Abbotsford Castle, near the River Tweed in Scotland. This, together with other unwise investments at a time of general economic depression, resulted in a debt which he spent much of the rest of his life paying off. Exhausted by his efforts, he died at Abbotsford on September 21, 1832.

1

In old times, a large forest covered the hills and valleys between the towns of Sheffield and York. Our story begins in this part of England when *King Richard I*, who had been away on a *Crusade* to the Holy Land, was being held prisoner in Austria. Back in England, rich 5 Norman *noblemen* were fighting each other to gain more power while the King was away. The ordinary Saxon people of England suffered in these *violent* times. They hoped that the King would soon return and bring peace back to the country. 10

One evening, just as the sun was setting over the forest, two men stood in a big *clearing*, complaining loudly about the Normans. The older of the two men was a *swineherd*. He looked very wild with his thick hair and large beard, and in his belt he had a long knife and a 15 horn. Around his neck he had a metal collar, like a dog's collar, on which it said, 'Gurth, the son of Beowulph, is born slave of Cedric of Rotherwood'. The other man was a *jester*. He wore a bright purple and yellow jacket and a hat with bells on it. In his belt he had 20 a wooden sword. Like his friend, the jester also had a

King Richard I, the King of England from 1189 to 1199, also called King Richard the Lionhearted

Crusade, in the Middle Ages, Christian armies went from Europe to the Middle East in order to fight against the Arabs for control over the Holy Land, Palestine

noblemen, rich people who have a title in front of their names, such as Lord, Sir, Duke, etc.

violent, with a lot of fighting

clearing, an open space in a forest

swineherd, someone who takes care of pigs

jester, someone whose job it is to entertain his master, see picture, page 6

5

jester

collar around his neck, with the words, 'Wamba, son of Witless, is the slave of Cedric of Rotherwood' written on it.

Suddenly, the two men heard the sound of horses
5 from among the trees behind them. A group of men came riding up to the swineherd and the jester. The first was the rich *Prior* Aymer, riding on a fat *mule*. Behind him came Brian de Bois-Guilbert, a Norman *knight*, who rode a big strong horse. He wore *chain-mail*
10 under a red *robe* with the white cross of a *Templar* on

prior, the head of a religious house, or priory, where monks live together
knight, in the Middle Ages, a noble soldier on horseback who serves a ruler
chain-mail, a kind of clothing made from metal wire, which knights wore for protection
Templar, a Knight's Order founded in 1118 to fight for the Holy Land

it. He was followed by several cruel-looking Arab servants carrying his *lance* and *shield*.

"Can you tell us the way to Cedric the Saxon?" the Prior asked Gurth and Wamba. "It is getting dark and we need somewhere to stay for the night." 5

"The road isn't easy to find, and Cedric goes to bed very early," answered Gurth.

"Don't argue with us, slave!" shouted the Templar angrily and was about to strike Gurth.

The Prior quickly stopped the Templar. "Now, 10 brother," he said to the Templar, "you must not think that you are still in Palestine!" With a silver coin in his hand, the Prior turned to Wamba instead. "Tell us, good fellow, how do we get to Rotherwood?"

Wamba told him which road to take to Cedric's 15 house and took the coin from the Prior's hand.

When the riders had disappeared into the forest

again, Gurth turned to his friend and said, "If they follow your directions, they will certainly not get to our
master's house!"

Wamba grinned. "No, but they may reach Sheffield
5 instead, which is a better place for them."

As the Prior and the Templar rode on in the forest, it
soon became too dark for them to see the road clearly.
They stopped to ask a man sitting by the side of the
10 road for directions to Cedric's house. The man said
that he would show them the way himself, and after a
short while they arrived at Rotherwood, the house of
Cedric the Saxon.

"Who are you?" Prior Aymer asked the man, whose
15 face was hidden by the *hood* of his robe. "You seem to
know this part of the forest well."

"I am only a poor *pilgrim* who has just returned from
the Holy Land," the man replied, and they went inside
together as it started to rain.

20 Cedric was a proud old Saxon with broad shoulders
and thick blond hair. He sat at the end of a heavy oak
table in the great hall of his house. Three big hunting
dogs lay at his feet. His men sat on long wooden *bench-
es* and ate their supper noisily. They knew that their
25 master was angry because his *ward*, the Lady Rowena,
was late for supper, and his swineherd and jester had
not yet returned from the forest.

Cedric was afraid that the two slaves might have

hood, the part of a robe or jacket that you can wear over your head
pilgrim, someone who travels to holy places
ward, a child whom you take care of, but is not your own

8

fireplace

bench

hunting dogs

been harmed by Reginald Front-de-Boeuf, one of his Norman neighbours. "Those Normans think that I am just a weak old man, but I will show them otherwise," he said to himself in a low voice. "Ah, Wilfred, Wilfred, my son, why could you not have controlled your 5 *passion*? And why did you go abroad to serve a Norman? You've left your old father alone to fight the Normans at home." He felt more sad than angry now. "And here come Prior Aymer and that Templar, Brian de Bois-Guilbert! Normans both of them!" he exclaimed when the guests were announced. "But I know my duty as a *host*. Tell them that they are welcome at Rotherwood! I've heard that priors and Templars are fond of drinking, so bring out our best wine for our guests!"

Cedric invited the Prior and the Templar to sit beside him at the head of the table. The pilgrim, however, said he preferred to have his supper standing by the great *fireplace*, away from all the other guests.

When Gurth and Wamba came into the great hall a little while later, the Templar recognized them from the forest. "You will die a violent death one day," he said to Wamba, "if you continue to give wrong directions to travellers like you did tonight."

"I only made a small mistake," the jester replied. "Someone who asks a fool for directions should be able to forgive that."

Their conversation was *interrupted* when another visitor was announced. It was Isaac of York, an old Jew, who had been on his way to Ashby and had come in from the storm outside. Cedric welcomed the old man, but none of Cedric's men would allow a Jew to sit down beside them. Only the pilgrim offered the old man some food and drink over by the fireplace.

passion, strong feelings (especially love)
host, someone who receives guests
fireplace, see picture, page 9
interrupt, come in between

When the Lady Rowena came into the hall at last, everyone stood up. She was a tall young woman with a beautiful face and clear blue eyes. The Prior noticed that the Templar was staring at her Saxon beauty. He warned the Templar that Cedric had *banished* his own son for looking at Rowena in the same way. Cedric had promised his ward to Athelstane of Coningsburgh, a Saxon of royal blood. Nobody else, not even his own son, would be allowed to marry her.

As she sat down next to Cedric, Rowena also noticed the Templar's look. She *blushed* and covered her face with a *veil*. "What is the latest news from the Holy Land?" she asked the Templar.

"Were there any knights who fought bravely at the side of our King?" asked Cedric. "Richard is a Norman, of course, but I'll have to forgive him for that."

"Yes," replied the pilgrim from his dark corner beside the fireplace, "there were many very famous knights who fought with our brave King, but none of them were Templars! One of the knights with King Richard was young and less well known, however, and I don't remember his name."

veil

---

banish, send away forever
blush, when your face becomes red because you are embarrassed

"I know who you mean," interrupted the Templar angrily. "It is Wilfred of Ivanhoe! If he were in England now, I would *challenge* him to fight against me in the *tournament* at Ashby in a few days. Otherwise, I will
5 call him a *coward* in all of Europe!"

"I will speak for Ivanhoe," said Rowena proudly, "and if he were here right now, he would accept this challenge and give this proud knight what he deserves!"

10 "Rowena," said Cedric, "let us not discuss these things now. Instead, everyone, let us all drink a cup of wine in honour of the Lady Rowena!"

Everyone raised their cups together with Cedric and cheered for the Lady Rowena.

2

15 That evening, when the guests were being shown to their rooms at Rotherwood, the Templar stopped the old Jew in the corridor.

"*Unbelieving* dog!" he said to Isaac. "So you are on your way to see the tournament at Ashby? I'm sure that
20 you have a lot of money hidden away somewhere."

"Money? But I am a poor man!" exclaimed Isaac. "Even the clothes that I wear are borrowed from a friend."

"*Liar*!" The Templar smiled sourly and turned to say

challenge, tell someone officially that you want to fight against them
tournament, a special event where knights fight against each other in front of an audience
coward, someone who is afraid to fight
unbelieving, not believing in Christ
liar, someone who doesn't tell the truth

something in Arabic to his servants.

Later that same night, Isaac woke up to find the pilgrim leaning over his bed. The pilgrim saw that the old man shook with fear and quickly said, "Don't be afraid, I have come to warn you! Your life is in great danger. I 5 understand Arabic, and this evening I *overheard* the Templar tell his men to kill you on the road to Ashby tomorrow. Let me guide you through the forest tonight so you can at least reach Sheffield safely."

The two men then went to the next room, where 10 Gurth, the swineherd, slept. "Wake up!" the pilgrim said to Gurth. "Open the gate for me and the Jew, so we can leave Rotherwood tonight."

Gurth was *suspicious*. "Like the other guests, you must wait till tomorrow before you can leave," he said, 15 as Wamba entered the room.

"I think you cannot refuse to do me this favour," said the pilgrim and whispered something in Gurth's ear. Gurth looked surprised and stared at the pilgrim. "But you must not tell anyone what I have just told you," 20 the pilgrim warned.

Gurth hurried to open the gate and let the pilgrim and Isaac out. He even kissed the pilgrim's hand before the two visitors disappeared into the forest.

"You know, my good friend Gurth," said Wamba, 25 who was *confused*, "you seem strangely religious today, kissing the hand of the pilgrim like that."

"You can't always judge people by their appearance,

overhear, hear something that you were not supposed to hear
suspicious, thinking that something is going on that you haven't been told about
confused, not sure of what is going on

13

Wamba," replied Gurth, and they went back inside.

Isaac followed the pilgrim through the dark forest until they arrived at the top of a small hill. The pilgrim pointed at the town of Sheffield below them in the
5 valley and said to the old man, "Here we part."

"Not until you have the thanks of a poor Jew," said Isaac. "Let me pay you for your kind help."

"I don't want anything from you," answered the pilgrim.

10 "Forgive me for guessing what you want most at the moment. You wish for a horse and *armour*."

The pilgrim turned and stared at the old Jew. "What makes you think that?"

"When you came to my room at Rotherwood, I
15 noticed that you wore chain-mail under your pilgrim's robe." Isaac quickly wrote some words on a piece of paper. "I have a rich friend in Leicester who will give you his best horse and armour if you give him this letter from me."

20 The pilgrim thanked Isaac, and they parted, each taking a different road down to Sheffield.

3

While King Richard was away, the two-day tournament at Ashby was a very popular event in England. Rich and poor, Norman and Saxon, came to see the best
25 knights in the country fight against each other in the

armour, the metal plates that protect a knight when he is fighting a battle

14

lists at Ashby. The winner of the tournament would have the honour of choosing the Queen of Love and Beauty from among the ladies present. The tournament was held by Prince John, the younger brother of the King, and the people cheered loudly when Prince John arrived and sat down in the royal *gallery*. What the people of England didn't know was that Prince John was secretly paying the Duke of Austria to keep his brother imprisoned. He and his Norman *allies* were planning to take the *throne* from his brother and make himself the King of England instead.

As he sat down and waved to the crowd, Prince John noticed that there was a loud discussion going on in one of the other galleries. Isaac of York had come to see the tournament together with his daughter, but the Norman noblemen in the front of the gallery were complaining loudly about letting a Jew sit next to them. Isaac knew that he had nothing to fear from the Normans, however, because Prince John and his allies were interested in borrowing a lot of money from the Jews of York. So he pushed his way through the crowd, while his frightened daughter held on to his arm.

"That *Jewess* is perfectly beautiful," Prince John said to Prior Aymer, who was sitting beside him.

"She is," agreed the Prior. "But, my lord, you must remember she is a Jewess."

---

lists, see picture, pages 16-17
gallery, see picture, pages 16-17
ally, person who is on your side
throne, the seat on which a king or queen sits. The throne is often used as a symbol for the whole kingdom
Jewess, a Jewish woman

gallery

lists

"Who is she?" the Prince shouted over to Isaac. "Your wife or your daughter?"

"My daughter Rebecca, my lord," answered Isaac.

Prince John looked up at the people seated at the

gallery

back of the Norman gallery. "Well, who is sitting over there at the back? Those *lazy* Saxons! Make room over

lazy, unwilling to work

17

there for my money-lender and his lovely daughter!"

The large Saxon man to whom Prince John had just spoken looked surprised at the Prince, but he didn't move. He was Athelstane of Coningsburgh, and although he had royal Saxon blood in him, he was known to be slow in both thought and movement, and many people called him Athelstane the Unready instead.

Prince John was *impatient*. "That man over there is either asleep or he is *ignoring* me!" He turned to a Norman knight sitting on a horse near the royal gallery. "Go and *poke* that lazy Saxon with your lance, De Bracy."

Maurice de Bracy rode over to the other gallery. He was just about to poke Athelstane, when Cedric, who was sitting next to the royal Saxon, jumped up and cut the tip of De Bracy's lance off with his sword. When Prince John saw this, he jumped up. He was just about to threaten the Saxons again, when he saw that the crowd was cheering and *clapping* for Cedric. One man, an *archer* who was standing near the royal gallery, was clapping particularly loudly. Prince John turned angrily to him and demanded to know what he was cheering for.

"I always enjoy a good fight," replied the archer.

"We shall see how well you do yourself, when we get to the archery competition at the end of the tourna-

---

impatient, feel that one has no time for small matters
ignore, not take any notice of
poke, give a push with something sharp
clap, make a noise with one's hands
archer, someone who shoots arrows (archery), see picture, page 33

ment," answered the Prince sourly and turned back to Cedric. "Meanwhile, you Saxons back there, stand up! The Jew has to sit among you! Let me see who dares to stop him!"

Cedric was certainly not about to let Prince John tell him what to do, and there would have been serious trouble if Wamba hadn't jumped in between his master and Isaac. "I will!" he shouted and swung his wooden sword over his head. Pulling back from the jester's sword, Isaac stepped back and fell down the steps of the gallery. The crowd, including the Prince and his Norman friends, laughed out loud at this sight.

"Give me a prize, Prince," said Wamba and came up to Prince John.

"Who and what are you?" asked the Prince, still laughing.

"I am a jester," answered Wamba. "I am Wamba, the son of Witless."

"Normans, make room for the Jew down in the front of the gallery," Prince John shouted over to the Norman noblemen. "Come here, Isaac, and lend me a handful of money."

Afraid, Isaac went up to the Prince and gave him the money from a little bag on his belt. Prince John threw the money to Wamba, and turned to the Prior. "We are forgetting the Queen of Love and Beauty! I hope it will be that beautiful Rebecca. That would really make the Saxons angry!"

"A Jewess!" Prior Aymer turned his eyes up in horror. "If Bois-Guilbert wins the tournament, I think I know who he will choose to be the Queen of Love and Beauty!"

Prince John gave the signal for the tournament to begin, and a *herald* came forward to read out the tournament rules. Five Norman knights had already been chosen by the Prince to be the 'challengers' for the day.

5 These five knights stood next to their tents at the end of the lists and held up their shields for everyone to see. According to the rules, these five challengers would have to fight against any other knight who chose to fight against them. A knight could choose to

10 fight against one of the challengers by touching that challenger's shield with his lance. If he touched the shield with the back end of his lance, the two knights would fight with their lances covered, so that there was no danger to the horses or riders. If the knight

15 touched the shield with the point of his lance, however, the knights would fight against each other with sharp weapons, like in a real battle. At the end of the fighting, Prince John would announce the winner of the day's tournament. The winner would receive a

20 war-horse as a prize and have the honour of naming the Queen of Love and Beauty.

On the second day of the tournament, all the knights would fight each other in two groups until Prince John announced the end of the tournament.

25 The Queen of Love and Beauty would then give a prize to the knight who had fought best on the second day. Finally, at the very end, there would be an archery competition.

The herald ended his announcement by shouting,

30 "Love of ladies - death of knights - honour and glory to

| *herald*, someone who announces things to the audience

20

the brave!" The audience cheered and threw gold and silver coins down to him.

At the far end of the lists, there were already so many knights on horses that the audience could only see a sea of shining *helmets*. With the eyes of the crowd on them, the first five knights rode forward to the tents of the five challengers. Each knight touched the shield of one of the challengers with the back end of his lance and rode back to the end of the lists. The challengers, led by the Templar, then *mounted* their horses and rode to the opposite end of the lists.

At the sound of the herald's trumpet the two sides *galloped* towards each other. The crowd heard the lances break and saw that the challengers had knocked four of the knights off their horses. The challengers rode back to their tents and the defeated knights dragged themselves out of the lists. A second and third group of knights came to fight against the challengers, but they were no more successful against the Templar and his fellow challengers. When the crowd saw that there were only three knights in the fourth group, they became very quiet, and whispered to each other that the Norman challengers were going to win the day's tournament.

 helmet

mount, get onto a horse's back
gallop, (of horses), running very fast

Cedric the Saxon was very unhappy with the outcome and he turned to Athelstane. "The day is against England, my lord," he said to Athelstane. "Aren't you going to take up your lance?"

5 "I will fight tomorrow," replied Athelstane. "It is not worth it for me to fight today."

"Yes, it is better, but not easier, to be the best man among a hundred, than to be the best man of two," said Wamba. Athelstane smiled at this, but Cedric
10 understood what the jester meant and gave Wamba an angry look.

"Are there any more knights who will fight against these challengers?" shouted a herald from the tournament lists, but no one came forward. Prince John
15 began to talk to his friends about giving the prize to Bois-Guilbert. With a single lance, the Templar had knocked two knights off their horses and broken the lance of a third. Trumpet music was already being played in honour of the successful challengers, when
20 suddenly a single trumpet could be heard in the distance. An unknown knight in full shining armour rode into the lists. On his shield there was a picture of a young oak tree pulled up by its roots and the word Desdichado, which is Spanish for *Disinherited*. The crowd
25 immediately started shouting to him which one of the challengers' shields he should choose, but the knight rode right up to Bois-Guilbert's tent and touched the Templar's shield with the point of his lance. This surprised everyone, especially the Templar himself, who
30 had been standing carelessly by his tent.

| *disinherited*, not allowed to receive (inherit) anything from one's family

"Have you been to *confession*, today," said the Templar, "since you don't value your life very much?"

"I am better prepared to meet death than you are," answered the Disinherited Knight.

"Then take your place and look at the sun for the last time, because tonight you will be sleeping in *Paradise*." 5

"And I *advise* you to take a fresh horse and new lance, for you will need both!"

Brian de Bois-Guilbert changed his horse and chose a new lance and shield. He did not want to take any chances against this unknown knight. The two knights then rode to the opposite ends of the lists. When the herald's trumpet sounded, they galloped towards each other with the speed of *lightning*. Both of their lances 15 broke at once, and the knights were given time to get new lances from their servants. The audience shouted wildly when they saw how well the Disinherited 10

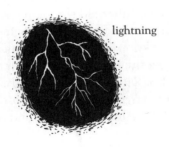

lightning

confession, when you tell a priest about the bad things you have done
Paradise, a place of perfect happiness where good people go when they die
advise, tell someone what you think he should do

23

Knight had done, but when the knights took their places again, there was a deep silence from the galleries, as if the crowd was afraid to breathe. This time, the Templar hit the centre of the Disinherited Knight's shield, and he would have won the fight if his own *stirrup* hadn't broken. Instead, he was thrown off his horse, and he fell onto the ground. Angrily, he drew his sword and waved it at the Disinherited Knight, who jumped off his horse with his sword already in his hand. They were stopped by two heralds who reminded them that the rules did not allow sword-fighting.

"We shall meet again where there is no one to separate us!" said the Templar angrily and walked back to his tent.

Prince John had no choice but to announce that the Disinherited Knight had won the first day of the tournament.

Two heralds asked the Disinherited Knight to take off his helmet in order to receive the prize from Prince John, but the Disinherited Knight refused. Prince John turned to his fellow Normans in the royal gallery. "Does anyone know who this proud man is?"

"It might be the King," said Waldemar Fitzurse, one of Prince John's closest allies. "It might be King Richard the Lionhearted himself!"

"What!" Prince John exclaimed and turned as *pale* as

stirrup

pale, white (of skin)

24

death. He shook as if he had been struck by lightning.

"It cannot be the King," said De Bracy calmly. "Look at him more closely, and you will see that your brother is a much bigger man than this knight."

Prince John could see that this was true, and he presented the war-horse to the Disinherited Knight. "Sir Disinherited Knight," he said, "since that is the only name by which we know you, you may now choose the Queen of Love and Beauty. If you are a stranger to our country, may I suggest the daughter of one of our Norman noblemen." He hung a gold *crown* on the tip of the Knight's lance. The Disinherited Knight rode straight past all of the blushing Norman ladies and stopped in front of the Lady Rowena, laying the crown at her feet.

"Long live the Lady Rowena, the Queen of Love and Beauty!" shouted the tournament crowd.

As he turned to leave, Prince John's eyes fell on the archer who had made him angry earlier. "Do not let that man leave Ashby," he told his guards angrily.

When the Disinherited Knight reached his tent, he spoke to his servant, a man in a big black robe.

"Gurth," said the Knight, "thank you for coming to help me here. I was afraid that someone might recognize you."

"I am not afraid of being recognized by anyone except my old friend Wamba," answered Gurth.

"Take this bag of gold to Ashby. Find Isaac of York and pay him back for the horse and armour."

crown, what kings and queens wear on their heads

25

Gurth took the bag and went off to the town of Ashby, where he found Isaac and gave him the money.

4

At sunrise the next day, the heralds were already busy writing down the names of the hundred knights who
5 were going to take part in the second day's battle. According to the tournament rules, the Disinherited Knight would lead one side, and the Templar, who was judged to be second-best in the fighting the day before, would lead the other side. Around ten o'clock, the her-
10 alds blew their trumpets to announce the arrival of Prince John.

When Cedric arrived with the Lady Rowena a moment later, he was very surprised to see that Athelstane had joined the side of the Templar. Athelstane
15 had secretly been very angry to see the Disinherited Knight choose Rowena as the Queen of Love and Beauty the day before. He was therefore determined to *punish* the Knight for this in the fighting. When Prince John saw that the Queen of the tournament had
20 arrived, he rode forward to meet her and led her to sit beside him in the royal gallery.

A herald read out the rules for the second day of the tournament: Apart from their lances, this time the knights would also be allowed to use swords and *bat-*
25 *tle-axes*. If a knight had been knocked off his horse, he could continue fighting on foot, but a mounted horseman would not be allowed to attack him. The fighting would stop as soon as Prince John gave the signal.

| *punish*, make someone suffer for doing something wrong

26

The knights rode into the lists and formed two groups of fifty men at opposite ends of the lists. They held their lances upright and the points shone brightly in the sun. When the heralds blew their trumpets, all the knights lowered their lances and galloped towards the 5 centre of the lists. The noise could be heard a *mile* away, and for several minutes no one in the audience could see anything through the great cloud of *dust* that had been raised by the horses' *hoofs*. When the dust had settled again, half of the knights were lying on the 10 ground. Some of them quickly jumped to their feet while others, who were wounded more seriously, were struggling to get out of the lists. The mounted knights, whose lances had almost all been broken, continued fighting with their swords, shouting out war-cries, 15 which were repeated by the excited audience. Soon their shining armour was completely covered in blood and dust. The ladies in the audience clapped and shouted, "Brave lance! Good sword!" to their favourite knights. 20

battle axe

mile, 5 miles is about 8 kilometres
dust, very fine pieces of earth
hoof, the foot of a horse

"Fight on, brave knights!" shouted the heralds. "Man dies, but glory lives! Fight on, death is better than defeat! Fight on, brave knights!"

As the lists slowly became less and less crowded, the audience could see that the Disinherited Knight and the Templar had finally met and were fighting each other. Front-de-Boeuf and Athelstane saw this too, and they rode up from behind the Templar in order to attack the Disinherited Knight from both sides at the same time.

"*Beware*! Beware, Sir Disinherited!" the crowd shouted out to the Disinherited Knight. Hearing them, he managed to strike at the Templar while pulling his own horse back sharply, thereby causing Athelstane and Front-de-Boeuf to ride into each other between himself and the Templar. As the three knights *recovered*, the Disinherited Knight rode off across the lists. Since he was riding on the war-horse that he had won the day before, he easily escaped from the Templar, whose horse was wounded, and the other two knights, whose horses were tired from the weight of their heavy riders. At the edge of the lists, he turned his horse around again and fought against all three knights with his sword. It was obvious to everyone, however, that he was *outnumbered* and would be defeated very soon. The noblemen around Prince John agreed that this was unfair and asked the Prince to signal the end of the tournament.

beware, be careful
recover, get well again
outnumbered, fighting against too many people at once

"No, by the light of Heaven!" replied Prince John. "This knight who hides his name has already won one prize. Now he should let others have their turn!"

During the battle in the lists that day, there had been a knight in black armour on a strong black horse who had started on the side of the Disinherited Knight. He seemed to take very little interest in what was taking place in the lists and carefully avoided fighting anyone himself. The audience thought he was being very lazy and called him the Black *Sluggard*. Suddenly, however, when he saw that the leader of his side was outnumbered, he shouted, "Desdichado, to the *rescue*!" and rode over to help the Disinherited Knight. With his sword, he struck Front-de-Boeuf so hard on the helmet that the Norman knight and his horse rolled onto the ground. Then the Black Knight grabbed the battle-axe from Athelstane and knocked the Saxon knight to the ground with it. Leaving the Disinherited Knight to take care of the Templar himself, the Black Knight then calmly rode out of the lists.

By this time, the Templar's horse had lost so much blood that it rolled to the ground. The Templar's foot was caught in one of the stirrups, and for a moment he was unable to free himself from the fallen horse. The Disinherited Knight jumped off his horse and waved his sword over the Templar's head, ordering the Templar to *surrender*. Just at this moment Prince John gave the signal for the battle to end.

---

sluggard, (old-fashioned) very slow and lazy person
rescue, save someone from danger
surrender, give oneself up

Prince John could not bring himself to announce that the Disinherited Knight had won the second day of the tournament as well. Instead, he suggested the winner should be the Black Knight, without whose
5 help the Disinherited Knight would surely have been killed. But the *mysterious* Black Knight could not be found anywhere, and Prince John had to announce the Disinherited Knight as the winner of the second day as well.

10 "Disinherited Knight," said Prince John, "since that is the only title you have given us, we now announce you as the winner of the tournament for the second day. You may now receive your prize from the Queen of Love and Beauty."

15 The Disinherited Knight rode over and got off his horse in front of the royal gallery. The Lady Rowena was about to place a crown on his helmet when a herald shouted, "This time he must take his helmet off!" The Disinherited Knight tried to stop him but he was
20 too weak. His helmet was removed by the herald, and the crowd saw the blond hair and bloody face of a young man of about twenty-five.

When Rowena saw his face, she cried out, and shaking, she placed the crown on his head. The Knight
25 bent down to kiss her hand but fell forward to the ground. The crowd cried out, and Cedric, who had been surprised at the sight of his banished son, rushed forward. The heralds, however, had guessed the reason for the knight's fall, and got to him first. They removed
30 his armour and found the tip of a lance in his side.

| *mysterious*, strange and unknown

30

The name of Ivanhoe flew through the audience, and it soon reached Prince John. "My lords," he said and looked around him, "I thought I felt the presence of one of my brother's knights."

"Now Front-de-Boeuf will have to give the land that you gave him back to Ivanhoe," said De Bracy.

"I have the right to *reward* my allies, instead of those who wander off to foreign countries together with my brother."

"Ivanhoe will not cause any trouble and won't want his land back from Front-de-Boeuf," said Waldemar Fitzurse. "I've just heard from the heralds that he is seriously wounded."

"Whatever happens to him, he is the winner of the tournament, and his wounds must be taken good care of!" Prince John added with an evil smile. "Let our own royal doctor take care of him."

But Fitzurse told the Prince that Ivanhoe had already been carried out of the lists by some of his friends. "I really *admire* the way the Lady Rowena hid her sorrow, when she saw Ivanhoe fall down before her," Fitzurse added.

"We shall *cheer her up* then," replied the Prince, "and marry her to a Norman. What do you say, De Bracy? How would you like to have her and her land?"

"She is very beautiful, and I would be happy to take her as my wife."

"Well, then she is yours, De Bracy."

reward, give something in return for something well done
admire, look up to
cheer someone up, make someone happy

A message was handed to Prince John by a servant. "Where is this from?" the Prince demanded.

"From abroad," replied the servant, and Prince John read it. "Beware, the *Devil* is free!" it said. The Prince turned pale and handed the message to De Bracy. "It means that my brother has been released from his prison in Austria," he added in a weak voice.

5

As Prince John recovered from the news of his brother's release, the trumpets announced the start of the archery competition, and more than thirty archers took their places in the lists. Prince John soon found the archer from the day before. "You! Come here! What is your name?"

"Locksley," replied the archer.

"Watch this man closely," Prince John said to his Norman friends. "See how his heart is sinking already. He knows he is going to lose the competition!"

A *target* was placed at the far end of the lists. As Prince John and Locksley watched, each archer shot three *arrows* at the target. At this distance, only ten arrows hit the target, but a man named Hubert hit the centre ring twice and was declared to be the best among them.

devil

"Now, Locksley," said Prince John, "will you try to compete against this archer or will you give up?"

"I will try on one *condition*: if I shoot at this man's target, he will have to shoot at my target afterwards."

"This is fair," said the Prince, and the target was 5 replaced with a fresh one. Hubert placed an arrow on his *bowstring* and took very careful aim at the target, measuring the distance with his eyes. He then took a step forward and drew the bowstring right back to his ear. The arrow flew through the air and hit the inner 10 ring of the target, but not exactly in the centre.

"You forgot to pay attention to the wind," Locksley said. "Otherwise it would have been a much better shot." While speaking, he walked up beside Hubert and

---

condition, what you want before you will agree to something

shot an arrow so carelessly, it seemed he hadn't looked at the target at all. The arrow landed in the target a bit closer to the centre than Hubert's arrow.

"By the light of Heaven!" exclaimed Prince John. "Shoot your best, man," he said to Hubert, "or you will be in trouble!"

Hubert stepped forward, and paying careful attention to the wind this time, shot an arrow right into the centre of the target. The tournament crowd cried out, "Hubert! Hubert!"

"You cannot shoot better than that," the Prince said to Locksley with an evil smile.

Aiming a little more carefully this time, Locksley *split* Hubert's arrow right down the middle. "And now," he said, "we will shoot at the kind of target that I am used to!" He went to a nearby tree and cut down a *branch* that was six *feet* long and as thick as a man's *thumb*. He placed it in the ground next to the other target and came back.

"I will not shoot at anything that I am sure to miss," said Hubert, looking at the branch. "I might as well shoot at a piece of *straw* or at a *sunbeam*, because I can hardly see that target from here!"

branch

thumb

split, break into two halves
foot, a foot is about 30 centimetres
straw, dried wheat
sunbeam, a ray of sunlight

34

"Cowardly dog!" said Prince John. "Locksley, if you can hit that, then I shall say you are the first man ever to do so."

"I will do my best," said Locksley and took careful aim at the branch. As the audience watched, he released his arrow and split the branch. Even Prince John had to admit that it was a good shot.

"You have won the archery prize," the Prince said, "and I will pay you twice as much if you will become my royal *bodyguard*."

"Pardon me, noble Prince," said Locksley, "but I have promised myself that if I ever serve anyone, it will be your royal brother, King Richard. Give the prize to Hubert instead. If he hadn't refused to shoot, he would have hit the branch as well."

Before Prince John could reply, Locksley disappeared into the crowd.

6

After the Black Knight had left the tournament at Ashby, he rode north for many hours through the great forest. Towards evening, the Knight started to look for a place to spend the night. The sun, which the Knight had used for directions, had already set behind the Derbyshire hills to his left, and it soon became too dark for him to see the forest road. Instead, he let his horse find its own way, and it took him to a little *hut* by a *stream*. Near the hut were the ruins of a very old *chapel*, where

bodyguard, someone whose job it is to protect someone else
hut, a small house, see picture, page 36
stream, a small river, see picture, page 36
chapel, a small church, see picture, page 36

hut

chapel

stream

the roof had fallen in long ago. The Knight got off his tired horse and knocked on the door to the hut.

"Go away, whoever you are," said a voice from within.

5   "Father, I am a poor traveller who is lost in this forest, and I would like to spend the night here."

"Go away, you are interrupting my *prayers*."

"The road - the road!" said the Knight. "Give me directions for the road, at least. That is all I expect."

10   "The road is easy to find. Go through the *swamp*, across the deep river, and then along the top of a *cliff*-"

"A swamp - a deep river - a cliff!" exclaimed the Knight. "What kind of directions are they to follow at night! Either open the door for me, or I will knock it

15   down myself!" The Knight kicked the door violently.

prayer, you talk to God in a prayer
swamp, a very wet area of land
cliff, a very steep hill

36

"Be patient, be patient," said the voice, and the door flew open. A fat monk rushed out angrily. When he saw the big man in armour in front of his hut, the monk politely invited the Knight inside and said he had been afraid that it was an *outlaw*. 5

The Knight looked around inside the hut. "You are so poor that outlaws cannot possibly be interested in stealing from you." The Knight took off his helmet, and the monk saw his thick blond hair and brave face.

"What is your name ?" the monk asked the Knight. 10

"I am known around here as the Black Knight. But some people call me the Black Sluggard."

The monk smiled at this and offered the Knight some dry bread and some water from the stream. He told the Black Knight that as a monk, this was all he 15 was allowed to eat. The Black Knight, who was very hungry, looked down at the food and back at the fat monk. "It seems to me that you are doing rather well on this. But I think there is some better food in this hut!"

The monk looked at the smile on the Knight's face 20 and went to get some better food and good wine. The Black Knight started eating and drinking while the monk watched. After a while the Knight looked up at the monk and said, "I have spent some time in Palestine, and it is the custom there that the host always eats 25 and drinks together with his guests."

"To make you feel better," said the monk, "I will forget that I am a monk and join you."

"Well, you certainly are the most mysterious monk I

outlaw, in the Middle Ages, a person who has broken the law and has to hide

37

have ever met," replied the Knight, but soon they were happily eating, drinking and singing songs together.

7

When Cedric saw his son fall down in the tournament lists, his first instinct was to tell his servants to go and
5 take care of Ivanhoe. But Cedric found he was unable to speak these words about his disinherited son in front of the crowd. Instead, he ordered his men to keep an eye on Ivanhoe and take him to the town of Ashby when the tournament was over. The servants found the
10 bloody spot where Ivanhoe had fallen, but they could not find Ivanhoe himself. They were told that a rich lady from the audience had arranged for him to be taken away from the tournament lists. Cedric was angry at this news, and the discovery that Gurth had gone miss-
15 ing during the tournament made him even angrier. He decided to return to Rotherwood that same evening together with the Lady Rowena and Athelstane. It was dangerous to travel through the forest at night as outlaws were known to attack and rob lonely travellers.
20 Cedric hoped that the outlaws, who were mainly poor Saxons themselves, would not attack fellow Saxons.

When the little group had travelled through the forest for a while, they came upon some mules and a *litter* on the road. Isaac was walking back and forth, *wringing*
25 his hands while his daughter sat next to the litter. Isaac quickly explained to them that he had paid some men to guide him, his daughter, and a sick friend back through the forest. Instead, the men had taken his

wring, to squeeze tightly

38

litter

money and horses and left them there on the road. "Please allow a poor Jew to travel with you!" he begged Cedric.

"We had better leave some of our servants with them to take them to the next town," Cedric said, and Athelstane agreed.

Rebecca, however, went to Rowena and said, "This is not for myself but for the sake of someone very dear to many, and dear to even you. Please, at least take the sick person in the litter with you."

"The man is old and weak," Rowena said to Cedric, "the woman is young and beautiful, and their friend is apparently very sick. We cannot leave them here."

Cedric agreed to let them travel with them, but Athelstane added, "They can only come if they travel right at the back of the group, where Wamba can protect them with his wooden sword."

39

"I lost my weapon in the lists like so many other knights," said Wamba, and Athelstane blushed because this had happened to him.

Slowly, the group continued together along the road in the dark, when they suddenly heard war-cries from every side. A group of men dressed in green rushed out from behind the trees. Cedric bravely swung his sword at them, but his sword hit a branch over his head, and he was knocked off his horse and taken prisoner. Athelstane was taken prisoner before he could even reach for his weapon. Of the others, Wamba alone escaped by quickly throwing himself off his horse and running as fast as his legs could carry him through the dark forest.

As he ran, Wamba suddenly heard a voice near him. "Gurth!" he cried out when he saw his old friend. "What are you doing here?"

"What has happened?" Gurth said. "What are these shouts and the sound of sword-fighting?"

"They have all been taken prisoner by outlaws! Our master was too ready to fight, Athelstane was not ready enough, and no one else was ready at all!"

"Let's rescue Cedric," said Gurth. "Follow me!" Gurth led his friend to a man who also wore the green clothes of an outlaw. Wamba recognized him as Locksley, the archer who had won the archery competition at Ashby. Gurth quickly explained what Wamba had told him to Locksley.

"Who is taking prisoners in this forest?" Locksley asked Wamba.

"I didn't see their faces, but they wore green clothes like yourself," answered Wamba suspiciously.

"I'll find out who they are. Stay here!" said Locksley

and disappeared into the trees. He came back after a few minutes. "I have seen the men. I know who they are and where they are going. Come with me, and we will rescue your master!"

The two men followed Locksley through the forest. 5 After three hours of walking, they came to a big clearing with a large old oak tree in the middle. Five men were sleeping under the tree while another man walked back and forth in the moonlight. The next moment, all six men had drawn their bows and were pointing their 10 arrows at Wamba and Gurth. When they recognized Locksley, they lowered their bows again.

"Where is everyone?" Locksley asked his men. "Gather as many of our men as you can find and meet me here again at dawn! Two of you go to Front-de- 15 Boeuf's castle, Torquilstone, and watch it carefully. Some men *disguised* as us are taking a group of prisoners there. Meanwhile, we three will go and get the monk." Locksley took Gurth and Wamba to the monk's hut. 20

Wamba looked at the ruined chapel and little hut in the moonlight. When they heard loud drinking songs coming from inside the hut, Wamba whispered to Gurth, "Is this where the monk lives? I never expected to hear such songs from a monk's hut at midnight." 25

Locksley knocked on the door of the hut.

"I hear some more guests, Sir Sluggard!" the monk shouted from inside. "They may be enemies of yours, of course."

"There are some people I would rather face with my 30

disguised, dressed up to look like someone else

41

helmet on," said the Knight. He laughed loudly while
he put his helmet on and picked up his weapons.

"Well, get your iron *pot* on your head then, Sluggard,
my friend!"

5   The two of them heard a voice from outside. "Mad
monk, open the door to me, Locksley!"

"All is safe - it's all right," said the monk to the
Knight and opened the door.

"We need every one of our men, *Friar* Tuck," Lock-
10 sley said. He looked at the Knight suspiciously. "Are
you mad, monk! You invited a Norman knight whom
you don't even know into your hut?"

"Not know him!" said Friar Tuck. "Why, I have
known him for a long time!"

15 "And what is his name, then?" asked Locksley.

"His name," said the monk, "his name is Sir Antho-
ny of Scrabelstone! As if I would drink with a man
without knowing his name!"

"You have already drunk more than enough, Friar
20 Tuck." Locksley quickly explained the situation to the
monk. "Therefore, we are going to attack the castle of
Front-de-Boeuf," he said.

"What!" exclaimed the Black Knight. "Is Front-de-
Boeuf taking prisoners in the king's forest!"

25 "Aren't you the knight who helped the Saxons

pot

---

friar, a kind of monk

42

against the Normans at the tournament at Ashby today?" Locksley asked. "I think you must be a friend of the poor and the weak. You are a friend of England. Will you help us attack Torquilstone?"

"I will! There is no one to whom England and the lives of every Englishman is worth more than to me," replied the Knight. "But who are you?"

"I am also a friend of my country," said the outlaw, and they set off together to meet the others back at the oak tree.

8

Meanwhile, the mysterious attackers were taking their prisoners through the forest. They did not know the way through the forest very well, and they got lost several times. As the sun rose, the two leaders of the attackers discussed their plans.

"Now you should leave us, Sir Maurice," the Templar said to De Bracy. "Then you can come back for the second part of your plan and rescue Rowena from her 'attackers'."

"I've changed my mind. I won't leave you until I have arrived at Torquilstone together with my prize," answered De Bracy. "Then I will go to the Lady Rowena and explain everything. I'm sure she will understand that I only did this because of my love for her."

"What made you change your plan, De Bracy? I hope you weren't suspicious of me? The Lady Rowena is very beautiful, but I have a prize among the prisoners who is as lovely as your own."

"You mean the beautiful Jewess! I would have thought you were more interested in the old man's

43

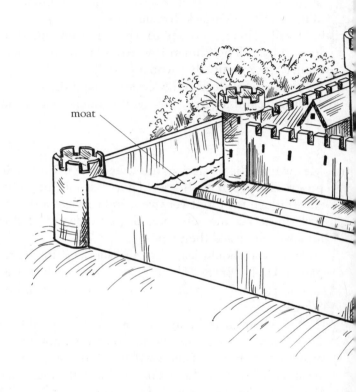

moat

money than in his daughter."

"Well, I like both. But the old Jew is only half a prize. Front-de-Boeuf is not lending us his castle for nothing, so I'm afraid we will have to share the old man's mon-
5 ey with him."

Soon they reached Torquilstone, the castle of

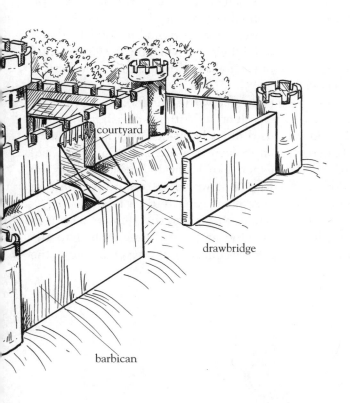

courtyard

drawbridge

barbican

Front-de-Boeuf. The castle was surrounded by a deep *moat*, which could only be crossed by passing through a *barbican* and going across a *drawbridge*. As the Norman knights came closer with their prisoners, the draw-bridge was lowered, and they rode into the *courtyard* of the castle. Here, the prisoners were separated and tak-

5

en to different parts of the castle. Isaac begged the guards to let his daughter go, but instead they took Rebecca away, and dragged Isaac down to the *dungeon*.

"I hope they won't forget to send us some food and
5 some wine," said Athelstane when he and Cedric were alone in one of the halls of Torquilstone. "I'm *starving* already!"

When a guard came with some food at last, Athelstane threw himself on it. With his mouth full of food,
10 he told the guard to let Front-de-Boeuf know that he challenged him to fight anywhere, anytime. "I would fight a dozen men like Front-de-Boeuf," Athelstane added to Cedric, "if it would get me out of a prison where they put so much *garlic* in their food!"

15 At that moment, they heard the sound of a horn in the distance. Cedric and Athelstane rushed to the window, but all they could see was the courtyard of the castle.

garlic

scale

dungeon, underground prison
starving, dying of hunger

46

In the meantime, Isaac of York was down in the dark dungeon of Torquilstone. It was very cold and *damp*, because the dungeon was deeper than even the moat itself. There were only two small holes at the top of the wall for air and light. Isaac could see a small fire burning in the far corner and some *rusty* chains attached to the dungeon wall next to him. In the dim light, he could see that there were two human legbones still in the chains. He sat down in a corner, folded his hands and waited.

Three hours later, he heard heavy footsteps outside the door. When he saw the large figure of Front-de-Boeuf standing in the doorway in front of him, Isaac started to shake with terror.

"I want a thousand pounds of silver," Front-de-Boeuf said with a deep voice. Slowly, the Knight came closer to the old man, and threw a *scale* at his feet. "Otherwise you will never be released from my dungeon."

"*Have mercy on me*, noble knight!" exclaimed Isaac. "I am old and poor and helpless."

"You may be old, but everyone knows that you are rich! Prisoners who were ten thousand times more important than you have died here in this dungeon. Can you see those iron bars over the fire in that corner? If you refuse to bring me the money, the guards will make you lie down on them as if it were a bed!"

Isaac looked over at the fire and back at the Norman knight. "That is impossible! The good God never made

---

damp, a bit wet
rusty, brown from water (metal)
scale, something used for weighing things with
have mercy on me, please don't hurt me

a heart so cruel!"

"Don't be so sure, Isaac," said the Norman with a cold smile. "Guards! Grab him!"

Front-de-Boeuf's guards came in and started to drag Isaac towards the fire.

"I will pay!" cried Isaac. "I will pay! I'll go and get the money in York, but let the other prisoners go first."

"No."

"Can I at least take my wounded friend with me?"

"No, Jew."

"Let my daughter go to York for me, then."

"Your daughter?" asked Front-de-Boeuf, surprised. "I wish I had known before that she was your daughter! I've already given her to the Templar."

Isaac cried out so loudly that the guards let go of him in surprise. Dropping to the ground, Isaac grabbed the knees of Front-de-Boeuf. "Take what you asked for - take ten times more - but let me keep my daughter! I will not pay anything unless my daughter is safe!"

"Are you mad? Aren't you afraid of the fire?" Front-de-Boeuf gave his men the signal to put Isaac on the red-hot iron bars. Just at that moment, they heard the sound of the horn in the distance. Voices from above called for Front-de-Boeuf, and the Knight told his guards to let go of Isaac and follow him upstairs.

9

At the same time, De Bracy had entered the room where the Lady Rowena had been taken. He greeted Rowena by taking off his *gloves* and large green hat and

gloves, what you wear on your hands

asked her to sit down beside him.

"If I am your prisoner, Sir Knight, I prefer to stand up," answered Rowena.

"Beautiful Rowena! You are not my prisoner - I am your prisoner! I have chosen you to be the queen of my heart. This has all been caused by your own beauty. Proud lady, I tell you, you will never leave this castle unless it is as Maurice de Bracy's wife."

"When I get married - should that day ever arrive - it will be to someone who does not hate the Saxon people like you do."

"I know what you're thinking, Rowena. Don't dream that Richard the Lionhearted will ever return, or that Ivanhoe will marry you instead! Ivanhoe is here in the castle, in my power."

"Wilfred, here? I don't believe you."

"Did you really not know this? Didn't you know that he was lying in the old Jew's litter? You know Front-de-Boeuf will kill Ivanhoe if he finds him here, because Ivanhoe will want his land back."

"Then save him, for the love of Heaven!" Rowena threw her hands up and started crying.

"I can - and I promise I will. I will hide him from Front-de-Boeuf," said De Bracy, *pacing* the room, "but then you must agree to become my wife. Remember that Cedric's fate also depends on you!" The distant sound of the horn interrupted him, and De Bracy rushed out of the room to find out what was happening.

In the meantime, Rebecca had been taken to a room in

| *pace*, walk back and forth

the highest tower of Torquilstone. She quickly saw that the room only had one, very large window, and that she had no way of escaping. The door opened behind her, and a tall man dressed in green came in. She held out some of her *jewellery* to him, hoping that this was what he came for.

"Beautiful flower of Palestine," said the outlaw in French, "I have always preferred beauty to jewellery."

"You are not an outlaw, but a Norman!" cried Rebecca.

"And you are so beautiful, one could almost think that you were a *witch*," said Brian de Bois-Guilbert.

"What do you want from me, except my money? We have nothing in common. You are a Christian and I am a Jewess. We could never marry."

"Marry? Marry a Jewess?" The Templar laughed. "I cannot marry anyone. I am a Templar!" He showed her the Templar's robe which he wore under his green disguise. "If it is necessary, I will take what I want by force. But if you take my religion, you can have a life with the best knight of the Templars. Most Norman ladies would be very *jealous* of you."

jewellery

witch

jealous, wanting something that someone else has

ledge

"Stand back! Take your religion? With **you** as the best knight, what kind of religion can that be?" As she spoke, Rebecca jumped up onto the window *ledge* and looked down into the courtyard far below. "God has given me a way to escape from this!" 5

The Templar was not prepared for this at all and had no time to stop her. He *hesitated* at first, afraid that she might jump if he came closer, but also because he admired how bravely she had jumped up onto the ledge. "Come down," he said, "and I promise by the 10 earth, the sea and the sky, that I will not harm you."

"I cannot trust you, Templar!"

"I promise by my sword, my name and my cross, I will not harm a hair on your head! I have broken many laws, but never my word. If not yourself, then think of 15

hesitate, not continue right away

your father! He will need a powerful friend in this castle."

"I will trust you - for now - but stay away from me." Rebecca stepped down off the window ledge, keeping her back to the window.

"Let there be peace between us," said the Templar. "Don't be afraid."

"I don't need to be afraid, as long as I have this window behind me."

"You are being very unfair to me, Rebecca," said the Templar. "Someone like you who is willing to die for her beliefs must have a proud and powerful soul, too. We belong together! No, don't be afraid. It will only be if you agree, and on your own terms. I have my *ambitions*, and one day I may become the Grand Master of the Templars myself! Just think of what this could mean for us!"

"What are you saying?" Rebecca asked, confused. "Do you really think -" She was interrupted by the sound of the horn in the distance.

"I must go now, Rebecca," said the Templar. "The others may need me."

When the Templar left, Rebecca knelt down on the floor and thanked God for her life.

10

The Templar and De Bracy found each other in the tower corridor, and Front-de-Boeuf came running up from the dungeon below. "Let us find out what this noise is all about," Front-de-Boeuf said. "Here, I've

ambition, wanting success or power

been given this letter, but I can't read it, because it is in Saxon." He looked at it, turning it round and round, as if he hoped the meaning would become clearer this way. Finally he handed the letter to De Bracy.

"It could be *magic spells*, for all I know," said De Bracy. "I never learned to read." 5

"Give it to me," said the Templar.

"What does it say?" asked De Bracy.

The Templar translated the letter into French, "I, Wamba, the son of Witless, jester of the noble Cedric of Rotherwood, known as the Saxon, and I, Gurth, the 10 son of Beowulph, the swineherd of Cedric, with the help of our allies, the good knight known as the Black Sluggard and the outlaw Locksley and his men, demand that our master Cedric the Saxon and the Lady Rowena and Athelstane of Coningsburgh, and 15 also the Jew, Isaac of York, together with his daughter, Rebecca, and certain horses, mules and goods, be delivered to us within an hour of receiving this letter. If you fail to do this, we will attack and destroy your castle." 20

At first the knights were lost for words, but then De Bracy burst out laughing. The Templar joined in, but Front-de-Boeuf looked impatiently at them.

"These men would not have written so bravely if they did not have a lot of men to back them up," said 25 Front-de-Boeuf. "There are a lot of outlaws out there in the forest who hate me. I've had as many arrows shot at me as that target at Ashby!" He turned to one of his guards. "Have you seen how many men are gathered out there?" 30

magic spell, secret words which make things happen in a way that is not natural

53

"There are at least two hundred men."

"Let us attack them," said the Templar. "One knight is enough for twenty such men."

"Enough, and too much," said De Bracy. "I am almost *ashamed* to use my lance against them."

"Send for help from your allies," said the Templar to Front-de-Boeuf.

"To whom should I write? All my allies are in York."

"Send a message to York," said De Bracy.

"And who shall carry the message? I know! Sir Templar, if you can write as well as you read, write a message to the outlaws for me."

"I would rather do it with my sword than with a pen," answered the Templar, "but I'll write it if that is what you wish." He sat down and wrote, "Reginald Front-de-Boeuf, with his noble allies, refuses to surrender to slaves. If the person calling himself the Black Knight is a real knight, then he should know he cannot demand this of good men of noble blood. Instead, we ask for a man of God to be sent to the prisoners to hear their confessions. In the morning, we will *execute* them and place their heads on the castle walls." The letter was then handed to the Saxon messenger waiting outside the gate.

In the forest outside Torquilstone, two hundred men were gathered already and more were arriving every minute. When Cedric's men at Rotherwood heard that their master had been taken prisoner by Front-de-

---

ashamed, embarrassed because what you have done is not honourable
execute, put to death, kill

Boeuf, they came in large numbers and joined the outlaws outside Torquilstone. The messenger passed
through the growing crowd and gave the Templar's letter to Friar Tuck.

"Why, this is in French!" the monk exclaimed and 5
passed it on to the Black Knight, who translated it into
Saxon for the rest of them.

"Execute the noble Cedric!" exclaimed Wamba,
when the Black Knight had finished. "You must be
mistaken, Sir Knight." 10

"If there were someone among us who could get into
the castle, he could find out how the castle is being
defended," said the Knight. "I think, since they ask for
a man of God, the monk should be sent in."

Friar Tuck refused loudly. 15

"Is there no one here who will go?" asked the Black
Knight.

Everyone looked at each other in silence.

"I see," said Wamba, after a short pause. "The fool
must be a fool and risk his neck when wise men refuse." 20

"Has he got enough sense to do this, do you think?"
the Black Knight asked Gurth.

"I don't know," said Gurth. "But if he hasn't, then it
will be the first time he has not been wise in his foolishness." 25

"*Pax vobiscum*," said Wamba, who was now wearing
the monk's robe, and he set off for the castle.

11
When the jester arrived at the gate of Torquilstone, the

pax vobiscum, (Latin) peace be with you

55

guard demanded to know who he was.

"Pax vobiscum," answered the jester, pulling the hood over his face. "I am a poor monk who has been asked to visit some prisoners in this castle." The guard let Wamba through the gate. When the jester was taken to Front-de-Boeuf, he shook with fear. "Pax vobiscum," he said weakly.

"Who are you, monk?" asked Front-de-Boeuf.

"Pax vobiscum," said the jester. "I was travelling through the forest when I was taken prisoner by outlaws. They sent me here to hear the confessions of some prisoners."

"Good," answered Front-de-Boeuf. "Can you tell me how many outlaws there are out there?"

"At least five hundred."

"What!" said the Templar, who came in at that moment. "So many!" He took Front-de-Boeuf aside. "Do you know this monk?"

"He is a stranger. I don't know him."

"Then don't tell him the message you want him to take to your allies in York. Let him carry a written message instead. In the meanwhile, let the monk wander around to see the prisoners, so that no one becomes suspicious."

The guards first took the jester into the hall where Cedric and Athelstane sat. "Pax vobiscum," Wamba said as he entered.

"Come in," said Cedric and looked up. "Why have you come, monk?"

"To prepare you for your death."

"That is impossible!" replied Cedric and stared at the monk. "They would not dare to kill us!" Then he became suspicious. "I should know that voice!"

"It is your jester!" answered Wamba, and pulled back the hood of his robe. "Put my robe on and leave the castle. I will stay here in your place."

"Leave you in my place!" exclaimed Cedric. "Why, they would *hang* you, my poor fool."

"Let them, my neck is too straight to be *twisted* by Normans."

"Save noble Athelstane instead, Wamba," said Cedric. "That is the duty of anyone who has Saxon blood in him."

"No, I will risk my life for whoever I choose."

"But the *ancestors* of Athelstane were once the kings of England!"

Wamba shook his head. "I will hang for no man other than my own master."

"Go, then, noble Cedric," said Athelstane. "When you are outside, you may be able to help our friends rescue us."

There were tears in Cedric's eyes as he put Wamba's robe on. "Farewell then, my poor boy," he said to Wamba. "I will either save you or come back and die with you!"

"Farewell, noble Cedric," said Athelstane. "Don't forget to accept any food or drink they may offer you on your way out."

"Farewell," said Wamba, "And remember, just say 'Pax vobiscum'."

Cedric pulled the hood of the robe over his face and

---

hang, kill someone by tying a rope around his neck and dropping him
twisted, bent out of shape
ancestor, person in your family who lived before you

hurried out of the hall. On his way across the courtyard, he met Front-de-Boeuf.

"Pax vobiscum," Cedric said.

"Have you prepared them for their deaths, monk?"
asked the Norman.

"Yes, I found them expecting the worst."

"Can you read, monk?"

"Not a word."

"Good. Take this letter to my allies in York. Say it
comes from me and was written by the Templar, Brian
de Bois-Guilbert. Also, see if you can find some way of
keeping those outlaws from running away when my
allies arrive."

"If I have anything to do with it, not a single Saxon
will leave the forest out there!" Cedric replied and
walked out through the castle gate.

Front-de-Boeuf turned to one of his guards. "Now,
bring me Cedric of Rotherwood and Athelstane of
Coningsburgh." Athelstane and Wamba were brought
in. "What have we got here!" Front-de-Boeuf
exclaimed when he saw the collar around Wamba's
neck.

"I think I can tell you," answered De Bracy as he
walked in. "This is Cedric's jester, the one who fought
so bravely against Isaac at Ashby. *Saints* in Heaven,
this must mean that Cedric has escaped in the monk's
robe!"

"What!" cried Front-de-Boeuf, looking at Wamba,
"I'll cut off his head and throw his body over the castle
walls!"

| *saint*, holy person

58

"No, give him to me instead," said De Bracy, "I'll give him to my men to amuse themselves with while they are waiting."

They were interrupted by the Templar, who came running down into the courtyard. He had been up on the castle walls, paying close attention to the *advance* of the outlaws towards the castle. "Those men are advancing with more *discipline* than I would have expected!" he exclaimed and they followed him back up. He pointed down at the edge of the forest. "See how well they use the trees for protection from our arrows? I think that they are being led by someone who has attacked castles before."

"I see who it is," replied De Bracy. "See that tall man in the black armour over there? That's the Black Slug-gard, the one who knocked you down at the tournament, Front-de-Boeuf!"

"Good!" said Front-de-Boeuf. "Bois-Guilbert, De Bracy, you can divide the rest of the attackers among you, but I will take care of that Black Knight myself!"

12

When De Bracy had left Rowena earlier, he ordered his men to take Ivanhoe to a safe place, as he had promised her. De Bracy's men took the wounded knight to Rebecca's tower room, which the Templar had told Front-de-Boeuf's men to stay away from.

Ivanhoe looked around in the tower room and immediately recognized the young woman who was

---

advance, coming closer, going forward
discipline, self-control

imprisoned there with him. "Thank you, dear Rebecca, thank you for saving my life!" On the way from Ashby, Rebecca had taken care of his wounds herself. It was only because of her great skills that Ivanhoe was now slowly able to recover his strength. "I see that we have been taken to the castle of Front-de-Boeuf," said Ivanhoe. "How can I protect Rowena and my father now?"

Rebecca told him that the castle was under attack from the outside. They could already hear the Norman knights shouting orders to their men in the courtyard below the tower. They heard the sound of armour and weapons being moved and the footsteps of men running to their places. Rebecca's face grew pale with fear, but Ivanhoe, who was used to battles, was impatient. "If I could only drag myself over to that window," he cried, "then I could see what was happening. If only I had a bow or a battle-axe!"

"Don't worry, noble knight," answered Rebecca. "The noise seems to have stopped suddenly. Maybe there will be no battle after all."

"You don't understand these things," said Ivanhoe impatiently. "That only means that all the men are in their places now and are ready to fight. If only I could reach the window!"

"You will only make your wounds worse, noble knight. I will stand in the window and tell you what I see."

"Rebecca, dear Rebecca, you must not!" exclaimed Ivanhoe. "The archers will be aiming at the windows-"

But Rebecca had already climbed up onto the window ledge. "I can see the archers standing in the shadows of the trees at the edge of the forest."

"Who are they?"

"I cannot tell. I can see a tall man in front wearing black armour. It's the Black Knight! They seem to be preparing to attack now. God protect us, what a terrible sight! The cloud of arrows is so thick that I cannot even see the men who are shooting them!" exclaimed Rebecca. "But wait! I see the Black Knight leading his men towards the barbican. They are running forward, but they are being forced back by Front-de-Boeuf's men! Front-de-Boeuf and the Black Knight are fighting each other now. He is down! He is down!" she exclaimed.

"Who is down?" cried Ivanhoe. "Tell me, who has fallen?"

"The Black Knight. But no - but no! He is up again, and fighting with the strength of twenty men. His sword is broken, but he has grabbed a battle-axe from someone else! He strikes Front-de-Boeuf - he falls, he falls!"

"Front-de-Boeuf?"

"Front-de-Boeuf," answered Rebecca. "His men, led by the proud Templar, are dragging him back behind the barbican. Now the attackers are placing *ladders* against the barbican walls. Great God! The ladders are being thrown down! The men are lying on the ground."

"Are they giving up?"

"No!" exclaimed Rebecca. "The Black Knight is striking at the barbican gate with his battle-axe. You can hear him over the noise and shouts of the battle! Stones and arrows are raining down on him, but he acts

ladder, see picture, page 62

61

ladder

as if they were *feathers*!"

Ivanhoe raised himself up. "I thought there was only one man in England who could do such a thing!"

"The gate has been broken down by him. They are
5 rushing in now. Oh God! They are throwing the defenders into the moat!"

"The drawbridge, have they crossed that yet?"

"No," replied Rebecca. "The Templar has destroyed it. A few of the defenders escaped with him back into
10 the castle. The cries and shouts you hear now are from the ones who did not make it back inside. I can see that the Black Knight is still fighting."

"By the name of the lady I love, I would gladly be a prisoner for ten years if I could just fight one day on
15 the side of that good knight in this battle!"

Rebecca came down from the window and sat down next to Ivanhoe. "You cannot hope to fight against

anyone as long as your wounds have not yet *healed*. Be
patient, my friend, I think the attackers will rescue us!"

feather

13

After their *retreat*, De Bracy and the Templar met
briefly in one of the halls of Torquilstone to discuss
their plans for the defence of the castle.   5

"Where is Front-de-Boeuf?" asked De Bracy. "The
men say he has been killed."

"He's still alive," said the Templar coolly, "at least
for a few hours more. But we have lost the barbican on
our side. How did the outlaws fight on your side of the   10
castle?"

"Like devils," answered De Bracy. "They are led by
that archer who won the prize at Ashby, and they have
already killed a lot of my men. If I had not been wearing Spanish chain-mail under my armour, that archer   15
would have killed me as well."

"Let us defend the castle walls!" answered the Templar, and they led their men to the top of the walls,
where they waited for the next attack by the outlaws.

Meanwhile, the outlaws met in the forest again to   20

healed, made well again
retreat, going back (opposite of advance)

make plans for the second attack. The Black Knight gave orders for some of the outlaws to cut down trees and build a floating bridge. When the bridge was finished, he turned to his allies. "We cannot wait any longer, my friends. The sun is already setting in the west, and the news of the battle may already have reached York. So, Locksley, take your archers to the other side of the castle and make it look as if our main attack is there. In the meantime, we will use the bridge from this side. Noble Cedric, are you with me? In the name of God, then, let us attack!"

As soon as the bridge had been pushed across the moat, the Black Knight and Cedric ran across it and reached the other side safely. Their position would have been more dangerous if Locksley and his men had not been shooting at the defenders from the other side of the castle. Three times Locksley shot an arrow at De Bracy and three times his arrow broke against the armour of the Norman knight. "*Curse* your Spanish chain-mail!" cried the archer.

"Shame on you all!" De Bracy shouted and looked around at the men who were left on the walls. "How can you let those two dogs stay down there on the floating bridge!" Suddenly he heard the Templar's voice in his ear.

"All is lost, De Bracy," said the Templar. "The castle is burning behind us."

"You are mad!" replied De Bracy.

"The west side is all in flames. I've tried *in vain* to put

---

curse, damn (word used when you are angry)
in vain, without success

64

out the fire."

"Saints of Paradise!" said De Bracy. "What is to be done now?"

"We will defend ourselves until our allies arrive. Take your men down and destroy the floating bridge. There are only two men on it at the moment. In the meantime, I will try to attack the outlaws over by the barbican."

"Templar, you won't let me down?"

"I will not!" said Bois-Guilbert. "But hurry up, in the name of God!"

De Bracy led his men down to the castle gate, but the Black Knight had already forced his way through it. De Bracy swung his sword at the Black Knight, and the Black Knight struck back at him with his battle-axe, knocking De Bracy off his feet.

"Surrender, De Bracy," said the Black Knight, bending over him and holding a knife against his helmet. "Surrender, rescue or no rescue. Otherwise you are a dead man."

"I will not surrender to an unknown knight," replied De Bracy weakly. "Tell me your name first."

The Black Knight whispered something in De Bracy's ear.

"I am your prisoner," De Bracy said to the Black Knight, "rescue or no rescue."

"Then go to the barbican and wait for my further orders," said the Black Knight.

"Let me first tell you that Wilfred of Ivanhoe is wounded and a prisoner here. He will die in this burning castle if you do not help him."

"Wilfred of Ivanhoe!" exclaimed the Black Knight.

"A prisoner! Tell me where he is!"

De Bracy gave the Black Knight directions to the room in the tower where his men had taken Ivanhoe. He then took off his helmet, gave his sword to Locksley, who came in as he went out, and walked across the floating bridge to the barbican.

Thick heavy smoke was already rolling into the tower room where Rebecca and Ivanhoe were imprisoned.

"The castle is burning!" cried Rebecca. "It is burning! What can we do to save ourselves?"

"Go, Rebecca, and save your own life," said Ivanhoe. "No one can help me now."

"I will not go without you," answered Rebecca. "We will be saved or die together. And yet, great God! My father - my father, what will be his fate?"

At this moment the door flew open and the Templar came in. "I have found you," he said to Rebecca. "You see that I always keep my word. I have cut my way through fifty dangers to take you to safety. Get up and follow me!"

"Go without me," answered Rebecca. "I will not follow you. If your heart is not as hard as your armour, save my old father and save this wounded knight!"

"A knight," answered the Templar calmly, looking down at Ivanhoe, "a knight, Rebecca, must meet his own fate, whether it is a sword or a flame."

"I would rather die in the flames than accept safety from you!" cried Rebecca.

"You have no choice," said the Templar and he picked her up and carried her out of the room in his arms, leaving Ivanhoe shouting behind them.

A few moments later, the Black Knight came into the room. "I would not have found you, Wilfred," he said, "if it had not been for your shouting!"

"If you are a true knight," said Ivanhoe, "then don't think of me. Go after that knight - save the Lady Rowena - find the noble Cedric!"

"In their turn," answered the Black Knight, "but it is your turn first." He lifted Ivanhoe up and carried him out of the room as easily as the Templar had carried off Rebecca. He left Ivanhoe in the care of some monks at a priory near the burning castle and went back to find the other prisoners.

One of the towers had completely disappeared in bright flames by now. Inside the castle, the air was filled with smoke and the sound of running feet and sword-fighting. The floors were wet with the blood of the wounded and the dead. In this confusion, Cedric rushed around with Gurth looking for Rowena. When he found her, he left her in the care of Gurth and ran on to try to find Athelstane.

Wamba and Athelstane had already made their escape and were standing in the courtyard of Torquilstone. Here they saw the Templar on his horse, surrounded by his Arab servants and defending Rebecca with his sword. The Templar attempted to cross the floating bridge, but his way was cut off by Locksley's men, who were shooting their arrows in through the gate.

Through the smoke, Athelstane saw a woman on a horse beside the Templar and thought it was Rowena. "I will rescue her from that knight, and he shall die by my sword!"

"Think of what you do!" cried Wamba. "She is not my Lady Rowena, look at her dark hair!"

But Athelstane had already rushed forward and knocked two of the Templar's Arab servants off their horses. "Come back here, false-hearted Templar! Let her go!"

"Dog!" said the Templar, turning his horse around. He stood up in his stirrups and struck Athelstane on the head with his sword. "Ha! That is what happens to anyone who challenges a Templar!" he shouted. "Those who want to save themselves, follow me!" He led his men through the rain of arrows, across the floating bridge and over to the barbican.

"De Bracy! De Bracy!" the Templar shouted when he reached the barbican. "Are you here?"

"I am here," replied De Bracy, "but I am a prisoner."

"Can I rescue you?"

"No, I have surrendered, rescue or no rescue. Save yourself. Put the sea between you and England! I dare not say any more."

"Well," said the Templar, "I will go to Templestowe for safety." He rode off into the forest, closely followed by his men.

The flames over Torquilstone rose up to the evening sky and could be seen for miles around.

14

By dawn the outlaws and their allies had all gathered back at the old oak tree. There they had slept, drunk wine and told each other stories from the battle. The money, armour and other *treasures* which they had taken from Front-de-Boeuf's castle had been thrown into a great pile under the tree.

"Let us not stay here long," said Locksley. "When the news of the battle reaches the allies of Front-de-Boeuf, we will need to find a safer place. Noble Cedric," he said as he turned to the old Saxon, "take half of these treasures and use them to reward your men."

"Good man," said Cedric, "my heart is heavy with sorrow. The noble Athelstane of Coningsburgh is no more. My hopes have died with him and can never return! The Lady Rowena wishes to return to Rotherwood right away. I have only stayed here to thank you and your men for saving my life. I am rich enough to reward my men with my own money." He turned and *embraced* his jester. "But you, my poor fool, how can I ever thank you?" Cedric's eyes filled with tears as he spoke.

"If you reward me with tears," said Wamba, "I shall have to cry as well. If you really want to reward me, forgive my friend Gurth, who left you to become the servant of your son."

"Forgive him!" exclaimed Cedric. "I will both forgive him and reward him. Kneel down, Gurth. You are now a free man, and I will give you some land of your own!"

Gurth jumped to his feet. "Someone help me take this collar off! Noble master, I will fight twice as bravely for you now!"

"But you will forget me," said Wamba.

treasures, very valuable things
embrace, take into one's arms, hug

69

"I will never forget you, my true friend," answered Gurth, "and if you wanted to be free as well, I know that Cedric would not stop you."

"I am not jealous of you," said Wamba. "I would rather sit by the warm fireplace in the hall of Rotherwood than in my own little house."

They were interrupted by the sound of horses, and the Lady Rowena appeared, surrounded by some of Cedric's men. Her face, although pale and sad, seemed to show new hope for the future. She knew that Athelstane was dead, but she had also heard that Ivanhoe was safe. She thanked Locksley and his men for her rescue. "*God bless you*, brave men," she said. "If any of you should ever go hungry, remember that Rowena has food. If the Normans should ever force you out of this forest, remember that Rowena has forests of her own."

"Thank you, gentle lady," said Locksley.

Before leaving, Cedric turned to the Black Knight and shook his hand. "Remember, you will always have a home in the halls of Rotherwood, noble Knight. Come, therefore, to Rotherwood, not as a guest, but as a son or brother!"

"Cedric has already made me rich," answered the Knight, "by teaching me the value of Saxon honour. I will come to Rotherwood some day, but I have more important things to take care of right now. When I come to see you, though, I will ask you for a great favour."

"You can have anything you want! Come to Coningsburgh, where I will be arranging the *funeral* of

---

| *God bless you*, may God take care of you

70

the noble Athelstane," answered Cedric and set off with the Lady Rowena and his men.

"Brave Knight," said Locksley, turning to the Black Knight, "take whatever you want from under this oak tree."

"I would like to take Sir Maurice de Bracy, to do with whatever I want."

"He is yours already," answered Locksley.

"De Bracy," the Black Knight said to De Bracy, "you are a free man - so leave England now! But beware of the future, Maurice de Bracy, beware!"

De Bracy bowed and disappeared into the forest.

Locksley gave the Black Knight a horn. "Noble Knight, if you are ever in danger in this forest, blow this horn and my men will come and help you."

The Black Knight took the horn and thanked Locksley for it.

"Long live our leader!" shouted the outlaws. "And long live the Black Knight!"

"Make room, men!" shouted Friar Tuck, who suddenly appeared with Isaac tied to the end of a rope. "Make room for your monk and his prisoner."

"Who have you got there?" asked Locksley.

Friar Tuck explained that during the battle he had been looking for the *cellar* in Front-de-Boeuf's castle, hoping to find some good French wine. Instead he had found this prisoner in the dungeon.

Isaac bent his head in fear. "For the love of God, will no one save me from this mad - I mean, this holy -

funeral, ceremony for burying a dead person
cellar, underground room in a house

71

man?"

"Were any of Front-de-Boeuf's men taken prisoner?" asked the Black Knight.

"No one very important," answered Locksley. "But we did find another monk in the forest on his way to Torquilstone. Here he comes now." Two of Locksley's men brought Prior Aymer forward to the oak tree.

"What is this, men?" demanded the Prior. "Are you Christians or Arabs, the way you treat a man of God? You have taken away my jewellery and torn my clothes! If you give me some of those treasures, I might forget this mad business."

Friar Tuck, who was still half-drunk, exclaimed, "Holy father, you are welcome in our forest!"

Prior Aymer looked at the monk. "What in Heaven's name is this? Please let me know how I can escape from these men!"

"You will have to pay us to be released, just like this Jew over here," said Locksley. "Can he afford it, do you think, Prior Aymer?"

"Can he afford it? Why, he is Isaac of York!"

"God help me!" exclaimed Isaac. "I am childless from this day. Oh Rebecca, my daughter! What wouldn't I give to know if you are still alive!"

"Wasn't your daughter dark-haired?" exclaimed one of the outlaws. "Didn't she wear a veil?"

"She did! - she did!" cried the old man. "Can you tell me if she is safe?"

"It was her, then," said the outlaw, "who I saw being carried off by the Templar's men. I would have shot an arrow after them, but I was afraid of hitting the girl instead."

"Oh!" cried Isaac. "Then I wish to God that you had shot your arrow! Her fate is now with that cruel Templar!"

"Friends," said Locksley, looking around, "this old man's sorrow has touched me. Isaac, take your money and see if you can buy back your child from the Templar. I hear that Templars love silver money as much as they love beautiful women. I cannot help you myself. The Templars' lances are too strong for my men. Let the Prior write a letter to Bois-Guilbert for you to take with you to Templestowe, the Templars' castle."

"Well then, Jew," said the Prior, looking around him at the outlaws, "since I must help you, can you find me a pen to write with?"

"I can find you one," said Locksley and shot an arrow at a wild *goose* which was flying over the trees that very moment. The goose fell down at their feet. Locksley pulled a feather out of the goose and gave it to the Prior. The Prior wrote a short letter to the Templar, folded it carefully, and gave it to Isaac. The Prior was then allowed to leave, and Isaac set off for Templestowe with the letter.

The Black Knight, who had been watching all this with interest, announced that it was time for him to leave as well.

goose

"Sir Knight," said Locksley, "we each have our secrets still."

"Next time we meet," said the Black Knight, "it may be without our secrets. Farewell, brave outlaw!" He rode into the forest, taking Wamba and Gurth with him.

15

At the Castle of York, Prince John met with the allies who were going to help him take the throne of England from his brother. Their plans had been delayed because Front-de-Boeuf, De Bracy and Bois-Guilbert were missing. Isaac of York, from whom they were going to borrow the money they needed to raise an army, seemed to have disappeared as well. On the morning after the fall of Torquilstone, *rumours* reached Prince John that the three Norman knights had been either killed or taken prisoner.

When he heard the news, Prince John paced the room impatiently in front of his allies. "Those cowardly *traitors*!" he exclaimed. "Those traitors, leaving me at a time like this. I should hang them from the drawbridges of their own castles!"

Just then De Bracy arrived to see Prince John. His armour was still covered in blood and dust from the battle at Torquilstone. He took off his helmet and placed it on the table beside the Prince.

"De Bracy," exclaimed Prince John, "what has happened? Speak! Are the Saxons *rebelling* against us?

rumour, general talk, gossip
traitor, person who secretly attacks his allies
rebel, rise up against a ruler

74

Where is the Templar? Where is Front-de-Boeuf?"

"The Templar has gone to Templestowe," said De Bracy, "and you will never see Front-de-Boeuf again. His grave is in the burning ruins of his castle. I alone have escaped to come and tell you this. But the worst news is still to come. Richard is in England, and I have seen and spoken to him."

"You are mad, De Bracy," exclaimed Fitzurse. "That cannot be!"

"There were only some outlaws with him, and even they don't know who he is," answered De Bracy. "I heard him say that he had to leave them, though. He only joined them to help them attack Torquilstone."

"What are you going to do?" asked Fitzurse.

"I? I am leaving for France at once."

"My good lords," cried Prince John. "As soon as Richard returns, you all leave me. And we are so close to winning everything now!"

"You don't understand," said De Bracy. "As soon as Richard returns, he will be at the head of an army, and it will be all over for us. I advise all of you to leave for France immediately."

"I don't need to save myself," said the Prince. "My brother would never harm me. But I must find him first!"

"Well, I shall not help you," said De Bracy quickly. "I was his prisoner, and he let me go. I will not harm him."

"Who spoke of harming him?" said Prince John, smiling. "No, we will just take him prisoner. Whether in England or in Austria, what does it matter?"

"I think the best prison is a grave," said Fitzurse.

"Prison or grave, I wash my hands of the whole matter," said De Bracy.

Prince John ordered Fitzurse to take his men and find the King. "They are going to take my brother prisoner," he said to De Bracy, when Fitzurse had left. "And I hope they will show proper *respect* for the life of dear Richard."

De Bracy only answered with a smile, and left.

16

In the meantime, the Grand Master of the Templars, Lucas de Beaumanoir, had come from Palestine and arrived suddenly at Templestowe. He had heard rumours about the Templars in England and had decided to come and see things for himself. The Grand Master was a thin old man with a long grey beard, but he still had the spirit of a fighter in him, and he was very angry at what he found at Templestowe.

"The Templars in England are even worse than those in France!" he exclaimed to his servant. "This is because they are richer. They do not take our battles in Palestine seriously, and instead enjoy themselves drinking, hunting and fighting here. I've heard people say that the Templars drink wine as if it were water. In England, it is apparently common to *boast* that one can drink like a Templar!"

A servant came in and interrupted the Grand Master. "There is a Jew standing at the gate who wants to speak to brother Brian de Bois-Guilbert."

---

respect, show that you value someone
boast, talk too proudly

76

"Send the Jew in."

Isaac came in and bowed deeply to the Grand Master. Then he folded his hands respectfully. He had heard that Lucas de Beaumanoir had been cruel to both Arabs and Jews alike in Palestine, and now looked at the Grand Master with great fear.

"What is your business with our brother Brian de Bois-Guilbert?" demanded the Grand Master.

"I have a letter from Prior Aymer for the good knight."

"Didn't I say these were evil times," the Grand Master said to his servant. "A prior sends a letter to a Templar and can find no better man to carry it than a Jew! Give me the letter!"

With shaking hands, Isaac unfolded the letter and was about to give it to the Grand Master.

"Back, dog!" shouted the Grand Master. "I will not touch unbelievers myself, except with my sword!"

The servant took the letter from Isaac and gave it to the Grand Master. He read the letter quickly, and a look of surprise and horror crossed his face. Then he read it again more slowly and turned his eyes up to Heaven. "When will You come and punish these *sinners*! Read it aloud," he said and handed the letter to his servant.

"Prior Aymer to Brian de Bois-Guilbert," read the servant. "I am a prisoner in the hands of some lawless and godless men. From them I have heard of Front-de-Boeuf's death and of your own escape to Templestowe together with that Jewish witch, whose beautiful eyes

sinner, someone who does something wrong in the eyes of God (commits a sin)

77

have *cast a spell* on you. I am happy to hear that you are safe, but warn you that the Grand Master is on his way to England to *interfere* with your plans. Make sure that he doesn't! As for the rich Jew who brought you this letter and is the father of the Jewess, make him pay you to get his daughter back, so we can enjoy ourselves with the money later. Don't forget to bring your wine cup! Till we meet again, Prior Aymer."

"What does he mean by saying that she is a witch?" asked the Grand Master. "Your daughter, Jew, is a prisoner of Brian de Bois-Guilbert?"

"Yes, sir," said Isaac, "and whatever I can pay to -"

"Peace!" said the Grand Master. "Your daughter is famous for healing wounds, isn't she?"

"Yes," said Isaac, proudly, "she is a very clever child, and many men owe their lives to her great skills."

"Ah, false Jew," said the Grand Master, "then she **is** a witch! I will teach her to cast spells on my Templars! Throw this old man out of Templestowe. We will deal with his daughter according to Christian law. Tomorrow we will have a *trial* here at Templestowe. If she really is a witch, her body will be burned at the *stake* and her *ashes* will be spread by the four winds! Bring me Malvoisin."

Albert de Malvoisin, the Templar in charge of Templestowe, came in and listened politely to the complaints of the Grand Master. "And finally, how can it be that you have a Jewish witch in this holy place?" the

cast a spell, make a magic spell work on someone
interfere, stop something from happening
trial, where a judge decides if someone has committed a crime
ashes, the powder that is left when something is burned

Grand Master shouted.

"A Jewish witch!" exclaimed Malvoisin, confused. He had helped Bois-Guilbert secretly hide Rebecca in Templestowe, but he was sure that no one knew of it. "Good *angels* protect us!"

"Yes, brother, a Jewish witch," said the Grand Master. "She was brought here by Bois-Guilbert. Have you got anything to say to this?"

"Well, that explains everything! I was wondering why so good a knight as Bois-Guilbert should be so fond of that woman. It seemed so strange to me, and I thought he was mad, but now you have let me understand that it was magic!"

"Maybe our brother Bois-Guilbert deserves *pity* more than punishment. I hear that he is one of the best knights we have! In Palestine, he killed over three hundred Arabs with his sword. Go and tell him of the news."

Albert de Malvoisin hurried out of the hall to warn Bois-Guilbert. He found him pacing his room angrily. "She still refuses me," said Bois-Guilbert. "Even though

stake

angel

pity, feeling sorry for someone

I risked my life to save her! The devil seems to be inside her!"

"The devil seems to be inside both of you," replied Malvoisin. "That old man Lucas de Beaumanoir has found out about your Jewess and says she has cast a spell on you. At least he pities you - to him, you are the *victim* of a witch - but she will of course have to die."

"She will not, by Heaven!" exclaimed Bois-Guilbert.

"By Heaven, she must and she will!" said Malvoisin. "Lucas de Beaumanoir has decided that her death will make up for all of our sins here at Templestowe. There will be a trial tomorrow. So throw yourself at the Grand Master's feet and tell him -"

"No, by Heaven! He thinks that she is a witch? Will future ages believe that such *prejudice* ever existed?" said Bois-Guilbert, pacing the room again. "Malvoisin, you are a cold-blooded -"

"Friend!" Malvoisin added quickly. "And let me give you some friendly advice: women are only for amusement. Ambition is the serious business in life. You could become the Grand Master yourself one day. Think of that!" He left the room to start preparing for the trial.

"Rebecca," said Bois-Guilbert, when he was alone, "why can I not leave you to your fate, as this *hypocrite* suggests? But beware, Rebecca, I will not risk my life and honour if you refuse me again!"

The trial of Rebecca began the next day at noon in the great hall of Templestowe. As Rebecca was led through

---

victim, someone against whom a crime is committed
prejudice, judging someone by their religion or race
hypocrite, someone who says one thing but does something else

the crowd, she felt a piece of paper being pressed into
her hand. When everyone had taken their seats, the
accusations against Rebecca were read out and the first
witnesses were questioned. Albert de Malvoisin had
worked very hard to find people who were willing to say 5
they had seen Rebecca practise magic. One by one, people from the neighbouring villages came forward and
said they had seen Rebecca heal the sick and wounded
with magic spells.

When the last witness had spoken, the Grand Master 10
ordered Rebecca to take off her veil. It was not the custom for the daughters of her people, Rebecca explained,
to uncover their faces in front of a crowd of strangers.
But she removed her veil, and the crowd cried out in surprise at her great beauty. The young Templars looked at 15
each other and knew that their brother Brian had been
a victim of Rebecca's beauty rather than of her magic
spells.

"I ask you, Brian de Bois-Guilbert," said Rebecca,
"are these terrible accusations against me not false?" 20

There was a pause. All eyes turned to Brian de
Bois-Guilbert.

"Speak," Rebecca exclaimed, "if you are a man, if you
are a Christian! Are these accusations true?"

"Answer her, brother," said the Grand Master, "if the 25
devil who is inside you will allow you to."

Bois-Guilbert's face seemed to show many different
feelings at the same time, and for a moment he was
unable to speak. Finally he looked at Rebecca and cried,

---

accusation, claim that someone has done something wrong
witness, at a trial, a person who tells what he has seen

"The paper! - the paper!"

"Yes," said Beaumanoir. "Here is the *proof*! The poor victim can only mention the piece of paper on which she has written her magic spells!"

5 But to Rebecca the Templar's words had a different meaning and she looked down at the piece of paper in her hand. On it was written, "Demand a *champion*!" in Arabic writing.

"Rebecca, have you got anything to say to this?" 10 demanded the Grand Master.

"I am *innocent*, and this accusation is false. I demand a *trial by combat* and thereby have a champion fight for my innocence."

"And who, Rebecca," replied the Grand Master, 15 "would fight for a witch? Who would be the champion for a Jewess?"

"God will give me a champion," said Rebecca and laid her glove down in front of the Grand Master.

"Brothers," said the Grand Master, looking around, 20 "we cannot refuse this woman her right to a trial by combat. Rebecca, daughter of Isaac of York, has challenged us to prove her *guilt*. Albert de Malvoisin, give this glove to Brian de Bois-Guilbert. I've decided that he shall fight against her champion for us! Rebecca, you have 25 three days to find yourself a champion."

"That is a very short time," answered Rebecca, "for a

proof, something that shows you what has happened
champion, here, someone who will fight on your behalf
innocent, not having done anything wrong
trial by combat, in the Middle Ages, a kind of trial where two knights, representing the two sides, fight each other and determine the outcome
guilt, having done something wrong

stranger to this part of the country to find someone to fight for her. But God's will be done!"

"How!" said the Grand Master, looking over to Brian de Bois-Guilbert. "Will he not agree?"

Albert de Malvoisin was still holding the glove and speaking to Bois-Guilbert in a low voice. "He will - he does," said Malvoisin, quickly putting the glove under his own robe. "And I suggest that the trial by combat take place right here in the lists outside Templestowe."

"Very well," replied the Grand Master. "Rebecca, if you fail to find a champion for yourself in time, you will die the death of a witch!"

Rebecca didn't speak, but folded her hands and looked up to Heaven. Then she quickly wrote a message on a piece of paper and handed it to one of the servants. "Find Isaac of York as fast as you can and give him this message!"

17

Later that day after the trial, Rebecca heard a low knock at the door to her room at Templestowe. When she saw Brian de Bois-Guilbert enter, she ran back into the farthest corner of the room.

"You have no reason to be afraid of me, Rebecca," the Templar said. "Do not think that I intended this to happen. I was only trying to save your life by rescuing you at Torquilstone."

"If you were trying honourably to protect the innocent, I might have thanked you!"

"Your words are bitter," said Bois-Guilbert, pacing the floor of her room impatiently, "but I haven't come to argue with you. Who do you think gave you that piece of paper telling you to demand a champion? I wanted to be your champion, but that old fool forced me to fight against your champion instead. Listen, Rebecca," said the Knight, coming closer to her, "if I go and fight in the lists, you will surely die. Ivanhoe could not possibly be strong enough to fight for you, and Richard is in a foreign prison. And yet, Rebecca," he threw himself at her feet, "I will give up everything and not appear in the lists, if you will only say that you love me!"

"Don't think of such foolishness, Sir Knight," said Rebecca. "Save me from this terrible death without asking for something from me in return!"

"No!" said the proud Templar, rising to his feet. "If I give up my ambition of becoming Grand Master, it will be for your love alone! We can escape together! Listen to me Rebecca," he added softly, "England - Europe - is not the world. I have friends in Palestine. We can go there together!"

"A dream," replied Rebecca. "Go and find King Richard instead. He will help me against these cruel men."

"Never, Rebecca!" said the Templar angrily. "If you refuse my love, I will still have my ambition. Ask Richard for help? Never, Rebecca! Farewell!"

18

When the Black Knight left the outlaws, he rode straight back to the priory near the ruins of Torquilstone, where he had left the wounded Ivanhoe. The two of them discussed some important matters, and the Black Knight sent messengers out in all directions.

"We will meet again," the Black Knight said to Ivanhoe as he got up to leave, "at Coningsburgh, the castle

84

of the dead Athelstane, where your father will be arranging his funeral."

"I want to come with you!"

"Rest today, Wilfred, otherwise you won't have the strength to travel tomorrow. I will take Wamba here as my guide."

"I fear you have chosen a *talkative* and troublesome fool to be your guide. But he knows every road in this forest."

Ivanhoe kissed the Knight's hand and watched him mount his horse. As soon as the Black Knight had left, Ivanhoe went to tell the prior that he would be leaving as well. Together with Gurth, Ivanhoe then set off on the road which the Black Knight and Wamba had taken into the forest.

On their way through the forest, Wamba sang happily for the Black Knight, and the Knight soon joined in himself.

"I wish, Sir Jester," said the Black Knight, laughing, "that Friar Tuck could hear your songs now."

"Unless I am mistaken, Sir Knight," Wamba said, "some men have been watching us from among the trees for a while. If they were friends, they would have joined us on the road."

At that moment three arrows hit against the helmet of the Black Knight. "What does this mean!" shouted the Knight angrily. The men that Wamba had seen rushed forward and attacked the Knight from all sides with their swords, shouting "Die!" A knight in blue

talkative, talking a lot

85

armour rode out from behind them and wounded the Black Knight's horse with his lance. The Black Knight fell to the ground and got up to continue fighting on foot. Seeing that the Black Knight was greatly outnum-
5   bered, Wamba quickly grabbed Locksley's horn from him and blew it with all his might.

The Blue Knight had already forced the Black Knight up against a tree and was about to kill him with his lance, when suddenly Locksley and Friar Tuck appeared
10 at the head of a group of outlaws. Within a few minutes, most of the attackers lay dead or wounded on the ground. Wamba ran up to the Blue Knight, who lay under his fallen horse, and pulled his helmet off.

"Waldemar Fitzurse!" said the Black Knight, sur-
15 prised. "What made you do this?"

"Richard," said Fitzurse, looking up at him. "If only you knew what ambition can make people do."

"Who asked you to become a traitor?"

"Your own father's son," answered Fitzurse.

20 An angry look crossed the Black Knight's face, but he calmed himself down again. "I will spare your life on one condition. Leave England and go back to your Norman castle within three days. Let him leave us unharmed, Locksley."

25 "I would have sent an arrow after him," said Locksley, watching Fitzurse leave, "and saved him the trouble of such a long journey."

"No. You have an English heart, Locksley," said the Black Knight, taking off his helmet, "and therefore you
30 must do what I say, for I am Richard of England."

As he spoke these words, the outlaws immediately fell on their knees in front of him and asked him to forgive them for the crimes that they had committed as outlaws.

"Rise, my friends," said the King, looking down at them. "Your crimes are forgiven through your *loyal* service to me at Torquilstone and here in the forest today. And you, brave Locksley -" 5

"You don't need to call me Locksley any longer, my lord. You can use the name which I am also known by: I am Robin Hood of Sherwood Forest."

"King of outlaws!" exclaimed the King. "Who has not heard of that name, from here all the way to Palestine! 10 Nothing that you have done in these troubled times while I have been abroad will ever be held against you."

"It is true what they say," said Wamba, "when the cat is away, the mice will play."

"Wamba," said the King, "your good service will not 15 be forgotten, either."

At that moment, two horsemen arrived. One was Ivanhoe on the prior's horse, and the other was Gurth on Ivanhoe's war-horse. Ivanhoe was surprised to see the group of outlaws and six or seven dead bodies lying on 20 the ground. He was even more surprised to see the King without his helmet on.

"Don't be afraid, Wilfred, to call me Richard in the company of these true English hearts," said the King.

"I don't doubt that," answered Ivanhoe, looking 25 around. "But what does this mean, these dead men and the blood on the armour of my King?"

"Traitors have been with us, Wilfred," said the King, "but thanks to these brave men, those traitors have met their deaths. But, I think you have been a traitor your- 30

loyal, supporting someone no matter what happens

87

self," he continued, smiling at Ivanhoe. "Did I not clearly tell you to rest in the priory until your wounds have healed?"

"They have healed," said Ivanhoe. "But why, noble King, do you trouble your servants by risking your life on lonely journeys and dangerous *adventures?*"

"Richard is prouder to fight when he only has his good sword," said the King, "than when he leads an army of a hundred thousand men into battle."

"But your kingdom, my lord," exclaimed Ivanhoe, "your kingdom is threatened by *civil war*. You are the only one who can unite this country. You owe that to your people!"

"My kingdom and my people!" answered Richard. "As I told you at the priory, I have to remain in disguise to give my allies in England time to raise an army. In that way, when the return of the King is announced, we will be able to stop any Normans or Saxons from rebelling against us." He turned to Robin Hood. "King of outlaws! Have you no food and drink for your fellow King?"

A meal was quickly prepared beneath a nearby oak tree. The outlaws hesitated at first at the idea of eating with the King of England, but he laughed and joked with them, and soon they happily joined him in the food and wine.

"We are honoured by the presence of our King," Robin Hood said to Ivanhoe, "yet we wouldn't want him to be delayed, if the kingdom is in danger."

"Well spoken, brave Robin Hood," said Ivanhoe.

adventure, dangerous and exciting experiences
civil war, when people of the same country fight each other

"Wilfred is impatient," said Richard, and decided it was time for them to leave. Robin Hood gave the King his hand, and Richard promised to help him in future, should he ever need the King's help. While the sun began to set over the trees above them, Ivanhoe, Wamba and Gurth set off with the King towards the Castle of Coningsburgh.

19

A large black flag was flying over the highest tower of the Castle of Coningsburgh. Inside, everyone was busy with the funeral arrangements for Athelstane. According to Saxon custom, *sheep* and *oxen* were being *roasted* in the courtyard. While the crowd of funeral guests ate and drank, jesters *juggled* and priests read out prayers. Gurth and Wamba quickly joined the guests in the courtyard, and King Richard and Ivanhoe went inside the tower. The King told Ivanhoe to keep himself hidden from his father until he gave the signal. Ivanhoe covered his face and stayed behind the King as they entered the main hall of the castle.

Here Cedric sat at the head of the table together with members of other important Saxon families. When he saw the Black Knight enter, Cedric stood up, raised his cup and sadly greeted him. The Knight and Ivanhoe followed Cedric to a small chapel in the castle, where they prayed for the soul of Athelstane. The Lady Rowena came in with some other guests and they sang a funeral

sheep, see picture, page 90
oxen, see picture, page 90
roast, cooked over a fire
juggle, throw things into the air and catch them again

song together. Cedric whispered to the guests that Rowena had been the intended wife of Athelstane. The old Saxon was about to leave the chapel again, when the Black Knight took his hand.

"I would like to remind you," the Knight said, "that when we parted, you promised me a favour."

"Of course, noble Knight," said Cedric. "Yet, at this sad moment -"

"I'm afraid I don't have much time. You have known me as the Black Knight," said the Knight, taking off his helmet, "now you may know me as Richard!"

"King Richard!" exclaimed Cedric, stepping back with surprise.

"Will you not kneel for your King?"

"I will never kneel for Norman blood," said Cedric.

"Wait, then, until I have shown you that I will protect Normans and Saxons equally well."

"Well spoken, Sir King," said the old Saxon. "For I will admit you are king, even though I don't like it."

"And now for the favour," said the King. "I ask you to forgive this good knight, Wilfred of Ivanhoe. I have an interest in the happiness of my friend, and in the friendship among my people."

"My father! - my father!" cried Ivanhoe, throwing himself at Cedric's feet. "Please forgive me!"

"You are forgiven, my son," said Cedric, helping him up. "I always keep my promise, even if it is to a Norman. You are about to speak," he added, seriously, to his son, "and I know what you are about to say, but the Lady Rowena must *mourn* for Athelstane for two years. The

mourn, be sad at someone's death

91

ghost of Athelstane himself would rise before us if we do not honour his memory!"

At Cedric's words, the doors flew open, and Athelstane came in, looking like someone who had indeed
5   risen from the dead! Cedric stared open-mouthed at the ghost. Ivanhoe prayed, and the King cursed loudly.

"In the name of God," said Cedric, "if you are human, speak! Alive or dead, noble Athelstane, speak to Cedric!"

10   "I will," said the ghost, very calmly. "Alive, did you say? I am as alive as someone who has lived on bread and water for three days can be. Yes, bread and water, Cedric! Thank God that I am here to tell you about it."

"Why, noble Athelstane," said the King, "I myself saw
15   you struck down by the Templar towards the end of the battle at Torquilstone. Wamba said that your *skull* was split right down to the teeth!"

"Well, Wamba was lying, Sir Knight," said Athelstane. "My teeth are fine, and I intend to use them on
20   my supper tonight. The Templar's sword had turned in his hand, and so he struck me with the flat side of his sword. As it was, down I went. I didn't recover my senses until I found myself lying in a *coffin* - an open one, by good luck! I *sneezed* several times and saw that I was in
25   the local church, not far from here. The priest came running when he heard me. He was not at all happy to discover that someone, from whom his church would

ghost, spirit of a dead person
skull, the bones in one's head
coffin, box in which dead people are buried
sneeze, sudden outburst of air through the nose (usually when you have a cold)

92

inherit a lot of money, was not dead after all! I asked for some wine, and he gave me a cup, but there must have been something else in it, because I slept for hours afterwards. When I finally woke up again, my hands and feet were tied, and I was in some kind of dungeon under the church. The priest came and gave me only bread and water for three days!"

"But noble Athelstane," said Cedric, grabbing the hand of his friend, "how did you escape?"

"I would be there still," said Athelstane, "if the chains that I was tied with were not so rusty that I could break them. I dragged myself upstairs as best I could and knocked the priest over the head. Then I grabbed some meat and wine and took the priest's best horse. I rode here as fast as I could. I only had a quick bite to eat before I came to find you, my noble friend!"

"And you have found me," said Cedric. "There has never been such a lucky day for the Saxon people as today!"

"I'm more interested in punishing that priest! He shall hang from the top of this castle. Why, Front-de-Boeuf was burned alive for a much smaller matter! He at least fed his prisoners well, only putting a little too much garlic in the food. But this *ungrateful* priest, who has often eaten with me at my table here in Coningsburgh, he only gave me bread and water - and he will die for it!"

"Noble Athelstane," said Cedric, "forget such matters and think of the future that lies ahead of you! Tell this Norman King that even though he may be lion-hearted, he cannot claim the throne of England as long as a true

ungrateful, not saying thank you

93

Saxon king is here to fight for it!"

"How!" exclaimed Athelstane. "Is this the noble King Richard?"

"Yes, it is Richard himself," replied Cedric. "But let me remind you that since he came here as a guest of his own free will, he may not be harmed or taken prisoner. Think of your duty as a host."

"Yes," said Athelstane, "and my duty as an Englishman! I promise to be loyal to you, Richard!"

"Think of the freedom of England!" exclaimed Cedric.

"Bread and water in a dungeon do wonderful things to a man's ambition! I rise out of the grave a wiser man than I was when I went into it. I have no interest in being king anywhere else than here, on my own land. And my first act as king will be to hang that priest."

"And my ward, Rowena," said Cedric, "you don't intend to leave her as well?"

"Cedric," said Athelstane, "be reasonable. The Lady Rowena does not care for me. She loves the little finger of Wilfred more than my whole person. There, she can tell you herself. No, don't blush, Rowena. Give me your hand instead. Here, Wilfred of Ivanhoe, to you, I will give - Hey! Wilfred has disappeared! Unless I am just weak from hunger, I am sure he was just here."

Everyone looked for Ivanhoe, but he was gone. They discovered that an old Jew had come to Coningsburgh asking for Ivanhoe. After speaking briefly to the old man, Ivanhoe had left the castle in a great hurry together with Gurth.

"Beautiful Rowena," said Athelstane, "I'm sure Ivanhoe had a very good reason to disappear like that -" But

Rowena, who had found the whole situation very embarrassing, had left the room as well. "Well, certainly women cannot be trusted!" exclaimed Athelstane. "To you I turn instead, noble King Richard, as a loyal -"

But King Richard was gone, too, and no one had seen 5
where he went. From Wamba, they later discovered that he had gone to find the old Jew who had come to see Ivanhoe. The King and the Jew had then mounted their horses and ridden off in the same direction as Ivanhoe and Gurth.
10
"I return from the dead," said Athelstane, "and everyone I speak to disappears as soon as they hear my voice. Come my friends, those of you who are left, and we will go to the great hall and eat before anyone else disappears!"
15

20

On the morning of the trial by combat, a great crowd of people had already gathered outside Templestowe. Every seat in every gallery was taken by people who had travelled for miles to see the exciting event. When the heavy bell of Templestowe began ringing, the crowd fell 20
silent and stared at the gate of the castle, hoping to see the Grand Master, the witch and the man who was her victim. The drawbridge of Templestowe was lowered, the castle gate was opened, and six trumpeters announced the arrival of the Grand Master. Behind him 25
rode Bois-Guilbert in full armour. His proud face looked very pale, as if he had not slept for several nights. After him came his Arab servants carrying his sword, shield and lance. Albert de Malvoisin rode at his side, and behind them followed the other Templars of Temple- 30

stowe and their servants. At the end came a group of
guards on foot. Among them, it was just possible to see
the pale figure of the accused woman moving with slow
steps towards her fate. All the knights entered the lists
between the galleries, and rode once around from right
to left. When they had made a complete circle, they
stopped, and all the Templars except Bois-Guilbert and
Malvoisin got off their horses and took their places in
front of the galleries. Rebecca was taken to a chair
beside a stake on top of a pile of wood. She looked at it
and closed her eyes in prayer.

"Lords and Grand Master," shouted Malvoisin, "here
stands the good Templar, Brian de Bois-Guilbert, who
must fight to show that this Jewess, Rebecca by name,
has deserved to die as a witch." He went over to the
Grand Master and laid Rebecca's glove at his feet.

The trumpets played and a herald came forward into
the lists. "Here stands the good knight, Sir Brian de
Bois-Guilbert," shouted the herald, "ready to fight
against any knight who will be the champion of the
Jewess." The trumpets played again and then there was
silence for many minutes as the crowd looked around
for the champion.

"No champion appears for the accused woman," said
the Grand Master. "Go, herald, and ask her whether she
expects anyone to fight for her."

The herald walked over to Rebecca's chair. "Girl," he
said, "the honourable Grand Master asks if you have
found a champion to fight for you, or if you confess your
guilt instead?"

"Tell the Grand Master," replied Rebecca, "that I am
innocent, and that I expect a champion to come and

fight for me, if God so wishes."

The herald went back and repeated her answer to the Grand Master.

"Tell her that we shall wait for a champion until evening," said the Grand Master. "If this day passes without the arrival of a champion, then prepare her for her death." The herald went back to Rebecca and gave her the Grand Master's message.

"Rebecca," whispered Brian de Bois-Guilbert when the herald had left again, "can you hear me?"

"I will have nothing to do with you, you cruel, cold-hearted man," said the unhappy girl.

"Yes, but do you understand my words, for my voice is frightening in my own ears. I hardly know why they have brought us here. When I look at the lists - this chair - that stake - I know what they are for, but it all seems so unreal to me."

"I know what it is all for. That stake is to send me, painfully, but quickly, into a better world."

"Dreams, Rebecca - dreams," answered the Templar. "Hear me, Rebecca, you have a better chance for your life and freedom than those fools over there know. Mount my horse behind me, and we will ride away from here! I don't care what anyone says!"

"Go away!" said Rebecca. "You will not change my mind. I am surrounded by enemies, but you are my most deadly enemy!"

Albert de Malvoisin, having discovered their conversation, quickly rode over to interfere. "Has the Jewess confessed her guilt?" he asked Bois-Guilbert. "Or does she insist that she is innocent?"

"She does indeed **insist**," said Bois-Guilbert sourly.

"Then come with me, brave Bois-Guilbert," said Malvoisin, leading Brian de Bois-Guilbert's horse away with him. "Come, you are the hope of the Templars, and you will be our new Grand Master one day!"

5   Everyone waited for another two hours. Just when the crowd was convinced that no one would come to defend a Jewess, two riders appeared in the distance. "A champion! - A champion!" a hundred voices exclaimed as a knight rode into the lists. But then they saw how tired 10 his horse looked, and how the knight hardly could keep himself in the saddle. The herald asked the knight to give his name.

    "I am a good knight and noble, and I have come to defend this lady, the daughter of Isaac of York, with my 15 lance and my sword."

    "The stranger must first show that he really is a knight," said Albert de Malvoisin. "The Templars do not fight against nameless men."

    "My name," said the knight, taking off his helmet, "is 20 Wilfred of Ivanhoe."

    "I won't fight against you," said the Templar in a quiet voice. "Get your wounds taken care of first, and get yourself a better horse."

    "Ha! Proud Templar," said Ivanhoe, "have you forgot- 25 ten that you have already fallen before this lance twice? Remember your challenge in the hall of Rotherwood! If you do not fight now, I will call you a coward in all of Europe!"

    Bois-Guilbert looked first at Rebecca and then at 30 Ivanhoe. "Dog of a Saxon! Take your lance and prepare yourself for the death you have brought upon yourself!"

    "Do you accept me as a champion?" Ivanhoe asked

Rebecca.

"I do," she exclaimed. "I do, I do accept you as the champion sent to me by Heaven! Yet, no - no - your wounds have not healed. Don't fight against this proud man! Why should you die as well?" 5

But Ivanhoe had already ridden to one end of the lists, where he put his helmet on and raised his lance. Bois-Guilbert slowly did the same at the other end, but his servants noticed that his face, which had been very pale that morning, was suddenly very red. Seeing that 10 each knight was in his place, the herald announced that the fight could begin.

The trumpet was heard, and the knights galloped towards each other. The tired horse of Ivanhoe went down, as everyone had expected, before the lance of the 15 Templar. But to the surprise of the crowd, the Templar, who had barely been touched by Ivanhoe's lance, also fell to the ground.

Ivanhoe, getting up from his wounded horse, placed his sword on the Templar's *throat*. He ordered him to sur- 20 render or die. Bois-Guilbert did not answer.

"Don't kill him, Sir Knight," cried the Grand Master. "He has been defeated." He came down into the lists and ordered Bois-Guilbert's helmet to be removed. The Templar's eyes were closed, and his face was still dark 25 red. As they looked at him, his eyes opened and his face turned the pale colour of death. Unharmed by the lance of his enemy, he had died, a victim of his own passions.

"This is indeed the judgement of God," said the Grand Master, turning his eyes up to Heaven. "I declare 30

| *throat*, see picture, page 100

throat

this young woman to be innocent!"

As the Grand Master spoke, they heard a low, *rumbling* sound and the ground shook under them as a large army of men rode into the lists.

5   "I am too late," said the Black Knight, looking around. "Bois-Guilbert was going to be mine to take care of!" He saw Ivanhoe. "Wilfred, was this a good idea, to come here when you could hardly keep yourself in the saddle? But we have no time to waste."

10   A knight rode forward from behind the Black Knight. Laying a hand on the shoulder of Albert de Malvoisin, the knight said, "I arrest you as a traitor. Your Templars have fought against the King in Palestine and in England."

15   The Grand Master stood up in surprise. "Who dares to arrest a Templar in the presence of the Grand Master?"

rumbling, a deep sound like thunder

100

"This knight arrests Malvoisin," replied the Black Knight, taking off his helmet, "by the order of Richard. Proud Templar, look up and you will see the English flag already flying over Templestowe instead of your Templar flag. Be wise, Beaumanoir, and don't try to fight against me! Leave England! Your hand is already in the lion's mouth."

"We will be back, Richard," answered the Grand Master proudly. He ordered the Templars to gather around him, and together they rode away from the lists into the forest.

Rebecca had neither seen nor heard the retreat of the Templars, for she was locked in the embrace of her old father.

"Let us go," he said, "my dear daughter - let us go and throw ourselves at the feet of that good young man who has just saved your life."

"O no - no - no," said Rebecca, "I do not dare to speak to him now. Otherwise, I might say more than - No, my father, let us leave this terrible place this very moment."

"But, my daughter," exclaimed Isaac, "they will think we are as ungrateful as dogs!"

"But you see," Rebecca said quickly, "my dear father, that King Richard is here, and that -"

"True, my wise Rebecca. Let us go - let us go! He has just returned from Palestine, and from prison, I have heard. He will be needing money, and he may decide to hold my business with his brother against me. Away, away - let us go!" Together, they quickly left the lists of Templestowe.

The crowd shouted, "Long live Richard with the Lion's Heart, and down with the Templars!"

"What is the news from York?" Ivanhoe asked the knight who had arrested Malvoisin.

"Our enemies are already leaving the country," said the knight, "and we have that news from John himself!"

5 "That traitor! That ungrateful traitor!" exclaimed Ivanhoe. "Didn't Richard put him in prison?"

"Oh! When they met, it was as if they had met after a hunt. The King just pointed at me and our army and said, 'You see, brother, I have some angry men with me.

10 So you had better go back to our mother and stay there for a while'."

"That was all he said?" asked Ivanhoe, surprised.

"Yes. Let us return to York," answered the knight, "for Richard will be punishing the traitors he has found, even

15 though he has forgiven their leader!"

21

While Maurice de Bracy and Fitzurse escaped to France, Albert de Malvoisin and many other Norman noblemen

20 were executed on the orders of the King. The King also ordered Cedric to come to York to help him get Saxon support there. Cedric did not refuse because he saw that Richard was a popular king, and he had no more hope for a Saxon kingdom. After a few days in York with

25 Richard, Cedric finally agreed to the marriage of his ward to Ivanhoe. He was secretly very proud of his son's adventures, and despite his feelings about the Normans, he soon became good friends with the King.

The wedding of Ivanhoe and Rowena was held in

30 York a few days later, and it was attended by a large number of Saxons and Normans, including the King himself. Gurth appeared in the church in fine new clothes at the

side of Ivanhoe, and Wamba arrived wearing a new hat with real silver bells on it. Everyone was happy that peace had finally returned to England.

On the second morning after this happy day, the Lady Rowena was told that a young woman had come to see her. Rowena was wondering who this could be, when a woman wearing a large veil entered. To Rowena's surprise, the stranger threw herself at her feet and kissed her dress.

"What does this mean?" asked Rowena. "Why are you doing this?"

"Because to you, Lady of Ivanhoe," replied Rebecca, getting up again, "I can show how grateful I am to Wilfred of Ivanhoe. I am the unhappy Jewess for whom your husband risked his life against terrible odds in the lists at Templestowe."

"Rebecca," said Rowena, "on that day, Wilfred only paid you back one small part of what he owed you for healing his wounds! Speak, is there anything I can do for you?"

"Nothing," said Rebecca, calmly, "unless you will say goodbye to him for me."

"Are you leaving England?" asked Rowena.

"My father has a brother in Spain. We will go there for peace and protection."

"Are you not well protected in England?" said Rowena. "My husband is a close friend of the King, and the King is a fair and honourable man."

"I do not doubt it," said Rebecca, "but the people of England are a war-like race, always fighting with their neighbours and with each other. This is not a safe place for my people. So farewell. Before I go, I have one last wish, though. You are wearing your wedding veil. I would like to see the face that I have heard so much about."

5 "I will remove my veil only if you will do the same," said Rowena.

They both took off their veils, and Rowena blushed deeply when she saw Rebecca's face. Rebecca also blushed, but only briefly. "I will always remember the
10 face which you have just shown me," she said. "It is gentle and good. I will now leave you with my rescuer -" Rebecca stopped as her eyes filled with tears. "No, I am well, - I am well. Please accept this gift from me." She gave Rowena a small box.

15 Rowena opened the box and saw that it was filled with beautiful jewellery. "It is impossible," she exclaimed. "I cannot accept such a valuable gift!"

"You keep it, my lady," said Rebecca. "Accept it - to me it has no value any more. I will never wear jewellery
20 again."

"Why, you are unhappy!" said Rowena. "Stay with us!"

"No, my lady," said Rebecca calmly. "Farewell. May He who made both Jews and Christians bless you." She
25 quickly left the room.

When the beautiful Saxon later told her husband about the meeting, it made a deep impression on him. Ivanhoe went on to live a long and happy life together with Rowena, for they had always loved each other. Yet
30 the memory of Rebecca's beauty and kindness came to his mind more often than his wife would have liked.

Questions

Chapters 1 and 2

1. Who are Gurth and Wamba? What work do they do?

2. Why does Wamba give the Prior and the Templar the wrong directions to Rotherwood?

3. What does the Templar tell his men to do to Isaac? Who overhears him?

4. Who do you think the pilgrim really is?

Chapters 3, 4 and 5

1. What is a tournament?

2. Why is Prince John paying the Duke of Austria?

3. Describe what happens when the Disinherited Knight meets the three knights. Who saves him?

4. What does the message that Prince John receives mean?

5. Describe what happens at the archery competition.

Chapter 6

1. Where does the Black Knight go after the tournament? How does he find the monk's hut?

2. Why does the Black Knight think that the monk must have some better food in his hut?

Chapters 7 and 8

1. What does Cedric do when he recognizes his son?

3. Why do Cedric and Athelstane think that they might not be attacked by outlaws in the forest?

4. Who attacks the travellers in the forest? What is their plan? Who is the only one to escape?

5. Describe the room where Isaac is taken.

6. What do they hear in the distance? What do you think it means?

Chapter 9

1. What does De Bracy tell Rowena about Ivanhoe? What does he promise her? What does he want her to do in return?

2. Why does Rebecca jump up onto the window ledge? What does the Templar think of this?

Chapters 10 and 11

1. Why can't Front-de-Boeuf read the letter from the outlaws? Why can't De Bracy read it? What does the letter say?

2. Who agrees to go to Torquilstone disguised as a monk? Do you think he is being brave or foolish?

3. Why have the Norman knights asked for a man of God?

4. What does Wamba suggest to Cedric? Does Cedric agree?

Chapters 12 and 13

1. Does Ivanhoe see the battle? How does he know what is happening?

2. What happens when Front-de-Boeuf and the Black Knight meet?

3. What does De Bracy tell the Black Knight? Why do you think he tells him this?

4. Who rescues Rebecca? Why does he leave Ivanhoe behind?

5. How does the Black Knight find Ivanhoe? Where does he take him?

6. Who attacks the Templar in the courtyard? Why? What happens?

Chapters 14 and 15

1. Why is Cedric sad after the battle? How does he reward Wamba?

2. What does the Black Knight want from Cedric?

3. Who is Friar Tuck's prisoner? How did he find him?

4. What does De Bracy tell Prince John? Where has he met King Richard?

Chapters 16 and 17

1. Why has the Grand Master come to Templestowe?

2. Why does the Grand Master think that Rebecca is a witch? What will happen to Rebecca if she is found guilty?

3. Why is Bois-Guilbert angry when Malvoisin comes to see him? Does he think Rebecca is a witch?

4. What happens at the trial of Rebecca? Is it a fair trial?

5. What does the Templar want from Rebecca? Does she agree?

Chapters 18 and 19

1. What happens to the Black Knight and Wamba in the forest?

2. What does Wamba mean when he says, "When the cat is away, the mice will play"?

3. Who appears suddenly in the chapel? Where has he come from?

4. Who arrived at Coningsburgh looking for Ivanhoe? Why do you think he came?

Chapters 20 and 21

1. What has the crowd come to see outside Templestowe?

2. Does a champion arrive to fight for Rebecca?

3. What is Bois-Guilbert's reaction to seeing Ivanhoe? What happens to him?

4. Why does Rebecca come to see Rowena after the wedding?

5. Why can Ivanhoe not forget Rebecca? Do you think this is a happy ending? Does everyone get what they deserve?

Activities

1. Make a list of the main characters in the novel. Whom do the following words describe?

good	evil	beautiful	brave
proud	cruel	gentle	kind
loyal	noble	rich	poor
wise	foolish	honourable	ambitious
Saxon	Norman	coward	traitor

2. Compare the following pairs of people. How are they similar? How are they different?

Ivanhoe - Bois-Guilbert
Rowena - Rebecca
King Richard - Robin Hood
Cedric - Athelstane
King Richard - Prince John
De Bracy - Front-de-Boeuf
Isaac - Cedric
Gurth - Wamba
Friar Tuck - Prior Aymer

3. A great number of people appear in disguise at one time or another in this novel. Who are they?